A NOVEL BY
DOUG JOSEPH

I0543230

Tesseract

BOOK TWO OF THE
SKYPORT CHRONICLES

WHITESTONE

PUBLISHING

STONEWOOD, WV, USA

Tesseract

BOOK TWO OF THE
SKYPORT CHRONICLES

Tesseract
Book Two of the Skyport Chronicles
By Douglas G. Joseph

ISBN-10: 1628830050

ISBN-13: 978-1628830057

Library of Congress Control Number: 2013957263

Printed in United States of America.

MEET THE AUTHORS, WATCH VIDEOS & MORE AT
WHITESTONEPUBLISHING.COM
THE SOURCE FOR GREAT CHRISTIAN READING

WHITESTONE
PUBLISHING
CHRISTIAN RESOURCES | INSPIRATIONAL NOVELS | CHILDREN'S BOOKS

For Elliana, Kieran, Adena, and Gavin

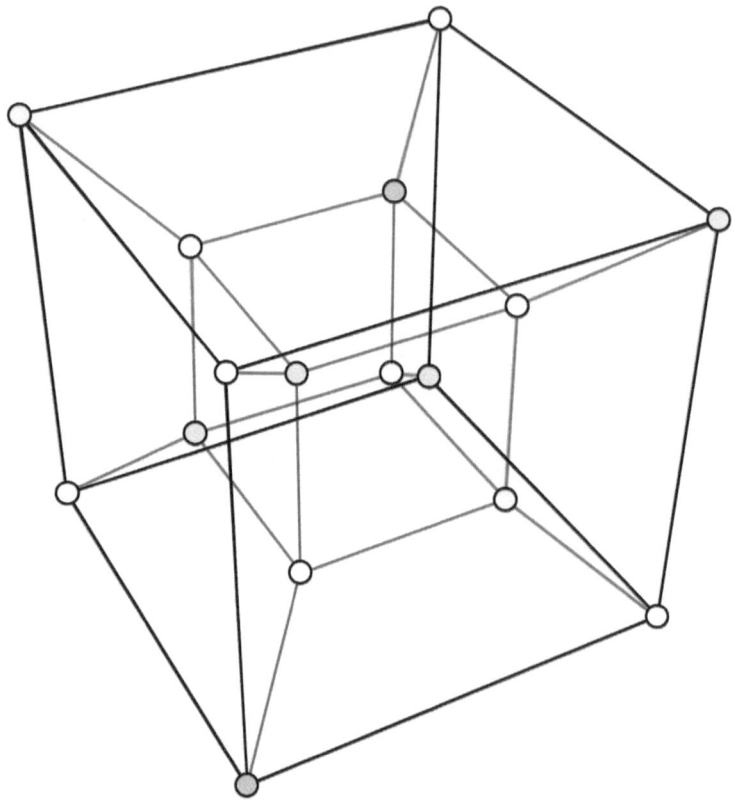

A *tesseract*, also known as a four-dimensional hypercube.
It is the four-dimensional equivalent of a normal cube.

CHAPTER 1

Tess

"Start strong, Tesseract." Her father's sentiment of wisdom, punctuated with a whimsical nickname, had been seeded in her spirit since before she was old enough to understand the words. He had occasionally repeated the phrase to Tess ever since her infancy, as if he could simply will his daughter to be strong even before she understood spoken language. He was a quiet, dedicated scientist. This encouragement to his only child later seemed almost prophetic. Indeed, she did start strong.

Tess was uncommonly bright. She began to speak in complex sentences long before she was two years old. Her vocabulary shocked everyone. Her rate of development was off the charts. Early grasp of communication skills was fairly common among girls, but not this early or this advanced. Over time, even more unusual developments were seen, such as her proclivity for mathematics and conceptualization of complex three-dimensional shapes and spatial relationships. The natural order was that everybody had a different mix of strengths and weaknesses in regard to academics. Yet Tess seemed to have no areas of weakness. She excelled in every discipline.

Despite how *Tess* sounds, it was no nickname. Although it is based on Theresa, Tess was actually her given name. (There was a bit of family history behind that.) Only her father called her Tesseract (a practice he began on the day she was born). Apparently her name reminded him of a certain theoretical concept, so he used it affectionately as a nickname. Her parents loved her greatly, and, unlike some fathers, hers was actually there for her.

They were people of very decent character, with strong moral values and high ethical standards (just as their parents before them were very moral), yet they, as a family, did not know God. Along with many others, their casual thinking was that the only goal and purpose of religion was simply to make people be decent and civil. Since they were already decent, they saw no need of it.

Because of the timing of her birth (she arrived late in the year) Tess was permitted to start school at a younger age than her classmates. Even then, she was already far better developed than they. All her teachers recognized her advancement potential. While Tess was still five, her first grade teacher arranged a chance for her to be enrolled in an accelerated program for gifted children. Of course, her parents, Perry and May, were agreeable, and she entered the accelerated program. Even that was not the least bit challenging for her. Thankfully she had an advantage greater than any school program; having a brilliant scientist for her father was a crucial aspect of her education. Indeed, the true foundation of her advanced development was not simply a transfer of facts and figures or modes and methods; it was that precious time in her formative years of having two loving parents who saw no limit to her potential, and who encouraged her often, yet without ever pressuring her. The transfer of content and concepts was second to none, but the hugs, I-love-you's, and other affirmations were the most effectual in her becoming a powerful person who also happened to be a great thinker.

Over the years her parents never asked her what she wanted to be when she grew up. As their friend, Roy, would say of them, they knew the difference between *being* and *doing*. While they occasionally mentioned possibilities for what she could *do*, such suggestions were not in the least connected with who she would *be*. Her parents shaped, and then trusted, who she would be.

At six years of age, Tess already understood spatial dimensions and rudimentary geometry. At that time her father decided to tell her about the theoretical concept behind her nickname.

"In advanced geometry," he said to her, "adding a theoretical fourth dimension—another *spatial* dimension, you understand; we're not talking about time—and then using this fourth dimension to generalize a regular three-dimensional cube into a four-dimensional shape results in a certain form of hypercube called a *tesseract*. The concept of folding the dimensions of 4-D space in a way that makes the tesseract's inner cube become an outer cube and an outer become the inner, has been used in science fiction to describe what is also called a teleport. When I was a child I read one science-fiction writer who used 'tesser' as a verb for teleport. Tesser just happens to be what my Mama, Theresa, actually called herself when she was small. That was eventually shortened to Tess, which is what everyone called your Grandma. When your Mama agreed to name you Tess in honor of my Mama, I decided right then and there that I would nickname you Tesseract. Sweetie, that is just your Daddy's way of saying that you can go to places no one has ever gone and do things no one has ever done. You're too young to understand it now, but one day soon I'll explain it to you better."

◆◆◆◆◆◆◆

Not long afterward, on the playground at school, Tess met a boy named Daniel Talbot, who was a little older than she was. They liked one another at once. (She was a little tall for her age, and he was a little short for his age, so they were well suited to one another.) Daniel was not in the gifted program, but Tess did not care at all about that. Daniel's father did not know God, but his mother did. The sanctifying influence of a saved, believing mother eventually became a very important help to Daniel and his siblings, but it was not in itself a redeeming help. Children born to redeemed believers are no more free from the sin curse than anyone else. Although they may have more knowledge with regard to truth and godliness, they still need salvation until they personally choose God and turn to Him for salvation.

With absolutely no pride and no sense of arrogance, Tess told Daniel, "My Daddy says I can go to places no one has ever gone and do things no one has ever done. He says I'm too young to understand it now, but one day soon he'll explain it better."

"Wow," Daniel replied, and he believed her at once.

Soon afterward, while the Talbots (Daniel and his family) were visiting some of their relatives, Daniel found a beautiful ring in the bedroom of his much-older cousin, Rick. Daniel wanted very much to give Tess a gift; to bring her something beautiful. There is no explaining why. It was as though such a desire was hardwired into his physiology. Being but a young child, he stole the ring. He knew of no other way to get her anything so beautiful.

The next day he approached her on the playground at school. Without a word, he handed her the ring. There was no box, bag, or bow. There was no explanation. At such a young age, who thinks of such things? Tess, being of an unusually advanced intellect, immediately thought of her mother's wedding ring set, and she thus connected a ring with marriage.

"Do you want to marry me?" she asked.

Daniel was too young to understand the ramifications of such a question, and he was not frightened even the least bit by the commitment that was implied.

"Yes," he responded with absolutely no guile.

Tess looked at the ring. It was far too big for any of her fingers, in the same way that marriage was far too big a concept for either of them. Yet there they stood on the school playground, mere children, staring at the ring.

"I'll think about it," said Tess. She accepted the ring from him and pocketed it.

"OK," said Daniel. After an awkward pause he asked, "So what did you bring for lunch today?"

"PB&J."

"Cool."

Neither of them paid any attention to a lady dressed in white who was watching them from the fence at the far edge of the school property. However, a teacher on duty, Mrs. Ronstadt, did notice. From a distance it looked to her like it might be Tess's mother.

"Tess, is that your mom?" the teacher asked, pointing toward the distant fence.

"Where?" shouted Tess, smiling as she turned to see.

Yet, to Mrs. Ronstadt's amazement, no one was there. She wrinkled her eyebrows in bewilderment.

"There was someone standing there a moment ago!" she exclaimed.

When the kids got home from school that day, neither of them mentioned anything to their parents about the ring. Also, neither one even gave a thought to the mysterious lady Mrs. Ronstadt had seen. Tess hid the ring in a secret place where she kept her dearest papers and most treasured toys.

At seven years of age, Tess drew on the sidewalk with chalk a shape somewhat similar to a hopscotch court. It was like a hopscotch court on steroids.

Her mother came along and said, "Oh, are you playing hopscotch? I've never seen a hopscotch game like this!"

"No," Tess said. "Look, Mama, I drew the net of a tesseract!"

May looked at the drawing and said, "The *what* of a tesseract? Did you say net? What do you mean, cutie?"

"I'm talking about the unfolding of a tesseract," Tess said, and she began to make motions in the air with her hands. "Just as a 3-D cube can be unfolded into six *squares*, a tesseract can be unfolded into eight *cubes*. Whenever you unfold a polytope the result is called its *net*."

May's eyes widened as her mouth hung open.

Finally she said, "Polytope? Unbelievable. Talking to my seven-year-old is like talking to a college kid."

Tess and Daniel had a friendship and trust that defied the popular myth that boys and girls are not attracted to each other until after puberty. While others were claiming that the opposite gender had "cooties," Tess and Daniel continued to talk to one another and spend time together on the playground.

As they got older, eventually puberty complicated matters, yet their friendship survived. Tess endured peer pressure regarding her friendship with Daniel. A snobbish boy in one of her advanced classes once said, "It's not that Daniel is dumb. He's just so *normal*. Wouldn't you rather hang out with someone who is closer to your own IQ?" Like everything else about her, Tess's response was mature beyond her years.

She replied, "My Dad says that many highly intelligent people are needlessly arrogant, and they cheat themselves out of having great friends because of their arrogance. He also says that having a high intelligence quotient does not mean anything when it comes to what makes people decent and good. Some smart people are not trustworthy. Some smart people are immoral and don't make good, faithful friends. Besides, if I decided that someone's IQ had to match my own before I would have them as a friend, that would leave you out. No offense. It's not that you're dumb. You're just so *barely above normal.*" She walked away thinking *Snob: rebuffed.* When her Daddy heard about it, he laughed and congratulated her. (He had always liked Daniel.)

Eventually Tess and Daniel had fewer and fewer chances to talk to each other. They were no longer at the same school. Daniel was passing through the normal school system as expected, while Tess was in a special pilot program that permitted advanced students to learn at their own pace, which, in Tess's case, was a blistering rate (she was on a schedule that would have her graduating from high school somewhere between 14 and 15 years of age). Nevertheless, they still felt like close friends. Tess never lost the ring he had given her previously. She thought of it often. She never wore it, though, because of the significance attached to it by the conversation they had as children.

Tess easily won all of her academic competitions. Several people told her that she could be the next Einstein. She appreciated her intellect for the blessing it was, but the pressure to become a world-renowned name in the history of science (even if the pressure was unintentional) bothered her. She loved learning for the sake of learning, and she won the academic competitions not because she was enormously competitive or desperate for recognition, but because it came easily for her. (She could only have lost if she had deliberately falsified her answers.) She sometimes felt badly for the older students (all of which were in high school) that she beat in those competitions, because it seemed to embarrass them greatly to be beaten by such a young girl. Several times Tess was featured in newspaper articles because of her academic prowess.

While Daniel was 14 years of age (in his freshman year of high school) and while Tess was 12 years old (but had already been working on high school-level courses for some time), it so happened that Tess knew in advance that on a certain occasion she was going to be at Daniel's school to take part in an academic competition. That day, before leaving home, she opened a drawer in her room and pulled out the ring. When she found him later that day, she approached him with the ring in hand.

After exchanging greetings with nervous smiles, Tess slowly opened her hand and showed the ring to Daniel.

"When we were little kids, you once told me that you wanted to marry me, and you gave me this," she said. Daniel didn't know what to say, so he said nothing, but the sight of the ring brought back such a flood of memories that he couldn't help but smile. Tess went on, "Back then I answered that I would think about it. Remember that?" Their laughter that erupted then was genuine, if nervous. Tess continued, "Well, as a little child I didn't know that a girl doesn't get to keep the ring unless she says yes. So I am here today saying, first, I'm not holding you to your declaration that day, and second, if that declaration is still good then I'm still thinking about it, and third, I can't keep the ring until I get to a place where I can say yes."

Daniel (who was no idiot) thought, *Wow*. Now, since human males often think and feel in ways that are not fully articulated (and usually even they don't understood what's going on within their own emotions), please allow this author to interpret for our fond reader what Daniel actually perceived. The fully detailed meaning of the simple *wow* would be something like this: *That's such a tactful way to bring up what could have been an awkward thing. She's so nice!*

Aloud he said, "Well, we were so little then; we didn't really know what we were saying. Now we're just barely old enough to know we're still kids. So I know we're not ready to tackle some questions, but...." He paused while he searched for the right words, and then he continued, "First, you're the kindest, sweetest girl I know, and second, you're the prettiest girl I know, and third, you're the smartest human being on the planet. I have nothing to offer that compares with what you deserve, but I'm going to go out on a limb and say that, from my side, the offer still stands—for whenever we're ready later—and that I'll be happy to hold your ring for you in hopes of getting a yes later." She smiled and nodded as he accepted the ring back from her, and after a pause that lasted long enough to become awkward, Daniel's keen sense of humor and excellent memory kicked in, which resulted in, "So what did you bring for lunch today?"

Tess also still remembered, and with a huge laugh she answered, "PB&J!"

"Cool," Daniel offered with a sigh of relief and more laughter.

They went on to enjoy their few minutes together. The time passed too quickly. Afterward, they began calling each other on the phone from time to time.

One night, later in that same year, the Addair's home phone rang. Tess's mother answered and then called to Tess, "It's Daniel calling for you, Tess!"

Tess grabbed the phone and said, "What's up, Daniel? Long time no see. It's great to hear from you!"

Daniel sounded somewhat apprehensive when he replied, "Tess, I have to tell you something. It's.... Are you sitting down?"

"What? What's wrong?"

"Nothing is wrong. You know how we've talked about God sometimes?"

"Right. I know your Mom is big into church and stuff."

"Tess, it happened for me. I was just filled with the Holy Ghost last night. This is real. The power of God is real. I was given a language to speak, so beautiful that you cannot even imagine it. This lasted for over an hour. It all started with me repenting. Then God filled me, and later I was water baptized in His name. All my sins are washed away! I'm saved now! I am part of the church!" There was a long pause while Tess tried to process what she had heard. Finally she spoke.

"Whoa. What sins were washed away? You're the most decent, good-hearted guy that I know. Why would you need to be saved?" There was another long pause while Daniel pondered her questions. Finally he answered.

"Well, for starters, when I was just a kid, I stole something valuable from my cousin's bedroom. It was a ring. You know the one I'm talking about. To this day I've never made that right with him. I actually stole several times as a child. Once I shoplifted a toy from a grocery store. I wanted the toy, and my Mom said no. So I hid it inside my coat sleeve and left the store with it. That night I broke two commandments, one against coveting and another against stealing. Another time I shoplifted some candy. Another time I stole some money from one of my relatives. The worst part is that I never even thought of all this until you asked me. I guess the Holy Ghost is bringing things back to my memory."

"Wait," Tess stammered. "You said that you repented. How did you repent if you didn't even remember what you had done wrong? And are you really thinking that God would send someone to hell for stealing candy, or for mistakes they made as a little kid?"

"OK, it's like this," Daniel offered. "Repent means to turn around. It means to go from not serving God, to serving God. It means to decide to stop being a sinner and to start being a believer who's trying their best to live right. I'm still new at having the Holy Ghost, but my Mama has taken me to church for my whole life. So I know some of this stuff. As far as God sending people to hell for childish mistakes, it's not like that."

"Well, how is it then?"

"It's more like this. What kind of person can steal from his own family, get past the guilt, have no remorse, and forget that he ever did it? Also, I've lied to people before—even my own family. I had never even thought of that until now. What kind of person can do that and feel no guilt over it? I've also gotten in bad fights with guys, including a couple of fights because they said something about you. Deep down I always considered myself to be a pretty decent person. Most of the time I have been, but there has always been a darker side. There has always been a serious problem with who I was—who I *really* was. I never even realized that the real me was someone entirely different than who I thought I was, and who I wanted others to think I was. I'm ashamed to say that. I was not who I thought I was—or who you thought I was.

"I think that a person can choose whether they want to spend eternity with God or without Him, but it's more complicated than that. Even getting to choose is a privilege we don't deserve, and people's default choice is eternity without God. The reasons are kind of hard to explain, but I will try. OK. You know how in the old days, back when there was slavery, the children of slaves were automatically born as slaves, too? Well, a long time ago, the first man and woman, Adam and Eve, decided to sin. They had been created in innocence, and they lived in paradise, yet they used their freedom of choice to sin against God. At that moment they brought a curse onto themselves. They became slaves to their new master: sin. All their kids were born as slaves to sin, too.

"That's why, when I was a little boy, no one had to teach me how to steal and lie. It came naturally. I was born as a slave to sin. Because I was a born slave, all real freedom was beyond my reach. I didn't even fully realize who and what I was. It was the kindness and mercy of God that allowed me the chance to become free and gain the realization afterward of all that had been wrong in me. A person who is still a slave often doesn't even know they're a slave, and they don't even fully know what is wrong in them that would cause them to reject God.

"We're all natural-born sinners from the time we come

into this world. We are born needing a change to take place. This business of hearing the truth and repenting—I mean turning around—and then being baptized and getting the Holy Ghost is when that change happens.

"God has told us that the penalty for sin has to be paid, and that penalty is death. So to have mercy on us, He came here and walked among us as the Son of God, so that He could die and go to hell in our place. Jesus paid the price for us by dying on the cross. He was buried, and His soul went to hell. But unlike us, hell could not hold Him. He rose from the dead three days later. We simply have to believe and then, with His help, make that change by obeying Him."

There was a short pause, during which Tess said nothing. Something in her was chiding that Daniel had gone crazy, yet part of her was mesmerized. She had never stolen anything that she could remember, but she was pretty sure that she had told several lies, even if she could not remember them at that moment. Part of her wanted to end the call, yet another part decided to give Daniel the benefit of the doubt. Daniel decided to continue. Because of the unerring accuracy of his words, she felt stung in her heart.

"When you hear me talk about the possibility of you having a relationship with God, which way do you want to go? Do you naturally want to shy away, say that I've gone crazy, and just leave God out? If so, what kind of person is that? What kind of person wants to run away from a loving God who is offering peace, hope, salvation, and eternal life? When you answer the question of what kind of person you are, if you find that you are a slave then you might realize why God does not so much 'send' people to hell as they rather choose it for themselves. He lets people have that choice to avoid Him for all of eternity if that is what they want, but He offers the freedom to want something other than that. We don't have real freedom of choice until we are given the gift of considering that there is more than one choice. The greatest freedom is no longer being a slave to sin.

"Please forgive me for not being more upfront about God before now. I was not the same person then, so I was simply wrong. I promise to try to be better. I—" Daniel stopped then. Although he wanted very much to say out loud for the very first time that he loved Tess, he was afraid that mixing that in with all the new information he had given her would muddle the real issue at hand and simply be too "over-the-top" in light of what had been said. Finally he simply said, "I just wanted you to know what happened."

Tess was completely speechless. Tess's parents were moral people, but they never talked about where their moral views came from. She had never thought about it. Tess's own moral views came from her parents. She accepted their values. Whether or not moral views that depended solely on one's upbringing could withstand the test of time was not a question she had ever considered. Something else she had never considered was how a Christian defense of the Holy Bible could withstand the anti-religious teachings of the neo-darwinist evolutionism being taught in their school courses.

Finally, in utter honesty Tess said, "I don't know what to say, and I am not sure what this means for us. I need some time to think."

"Well," Daniel answered, "that is a perfectly intelligent way to answer. In fact I think it's wonderful that although I've dropped a bombshell on you that's bigger than saying I want to marry you, your answer is still the same: you will think about it. One thing I have learned is that whenever you think about things, usually you come up with the right answer. I'm happy to give you time to think."

There was not any reason to try to make small talk as though the call had not gone the way it had. They both politely said goodbye. Daniel sighed, and wondered if she would ever turn to God or even have anything to do with him ever again.

In the days and weeks that followed, Tess simply put the conversation out of her mind. She stopped calling Daniel, and he, taking the hint, did not bother her. Thus began a period in which they had no contact with each other. For the first time since they met, they did not know whether they were still friends or not.

The following year, Daniel recognized that he was called to preach. Since he and Tess were not communicating, she had no idea that he preached his first sermon at 16 years of age.

At 14 years of age, Tess graduated from high school, with over a year's worth of college credits already completed. She was the youngest high school graduate in the state's history. Daniel was finishing his sophomore year of high school. He attended her graduation and cheered her on. After the ceremony, he came and congratulated her in person. It was the first time they had spoken to each other in many months, and it was the first time they had seen each other face to face in two years.

Daniel was awestruck by how beautiful Tess had become. Tess was secretly overwhelmed by how handsome Daniel was, and she took note of how much more confident and at ease he was around people. She was genuinely glad to see him, and she thoroughly hoped that he would not start with the religious questions again. He did not.

They spoke for several wonderful minutes and exchanged cell numbers. It was bittersweet when they parted that day. They each wanted to find a way to continue their relationship, yet Tess's unanswered questions about God meant that they could have no solid plan for where to go from there.

◆◆◆◆◆◆◆

Tess used the College-Level Examination Program (CLEP) to obtain a few more college credits. Then she attended college while still living with her parents at home. She got her first college degree at 16 years of age, just as Daniel was graduating from high school. No one had ever heard of anyone graduating from college so young.

In the weeks leading up to Tess's commencement ceremonies, God tried to warn her family that danger was ahead; that something was wrong and needed to be taken care of. However, because they were unredeemed people that had no relationship with the Lord, they mistook His nudges as simply them having irrational feelings of having forgotten something. Tess's mother and father asked each other, as well as Tess, what they were forgetting. Tess's mother felt overwhelmed at times by a gnawing sense of dread. They all simply shrugged it off. They did not know what else to do.

What happened soon afterward was terrible beyond description, and no one saw it coming except for God and one handsome boy who was open to hearing God's voice foretell it.

The night before Tess's commencement, the Lord tried to forewarn Daniel in a dream, but he simply was unable to accept it until the Lord spoke to him even more strongly the next day.

CHAPTER II

Degree of Suffering

Finally, Tess's degree day had arrived. It was her much anticipated commencement. Tess and her parents were excited, and they fussed over every detail. They struggled to leave the house on time. Eventually they managed to make it into the car, but they would have to hurry to get to the ceremonies in time.

Tess's parents were not wealthy. They were exceptional people who lived very modestly. Times were tight, and their vehicles were not new models, to say the least. They did not know that a corroded brake line was about to burst in their aged, midsize sedan. They did not know that a disastrous set of events was about to unfold. The Lord had continued to warn Daniel until finally he understood that he needed to make a call.

Tess's cell phone rang. It was Daniel. She was elated to hear from him.

"Hey, Dan! It's my big day! Are you excited? You're coming, right?"

"Tess, I have bad news. I was praying, and I felt like God told me to tell you not to go. Something bad will happen. Don't go."

"What? Don't go where?"

"Don't go to the ceremony. Don't go."

"I cannot believe what I am hearing. You gotta be kidding me. This is a joke, right?"

"No joke. I am dead serious. Can I talk to your Dad?"

Tess put the phone against her knee and said, "Dad, Daniel is on the phone. He's talking crazy. He wants to talk to you. He is saying God told him something bad will happen to us if we go to the ceremonies today."

Her father said, "Well, I'm driving, and if I talk on a cell phone something bad may happen. Let Mama talk to him."

He was indeed driving like a maniac. Tess gave the phone to her mother.

"Hello."

"Mrs. Addair?"

"Yes, Daniel?"

"Hi. I know this sounds crazy, but you've known me practically my whole life. You know I'm not crazy. Something bad is going to happen if you keep going. I am begging you in the name of Jesus. Please stop. Turn around. Please don't go to the ceremony today."

Daniel's use of the Lord's name in that certain way caused a renewed sense of dread to sweep over her. She tried in vain to just shake it off, but she still refused to heed the warning.

"Well," she said, "the way my husband is driving, I feel like we are in danger. Look, Daniel, we cannot avoid the ceremonies today, but I will promise you that I will make my husband slow down, OK?"

"But—" Daniel tried to say more, but she cut him off.

"Listen, Daniel, you know that we think you are a fine young man, but you have to understand what a big day this is for Tess, OK? We'll see you there, I hope. Bye now."

As soon as she ended the call, Perry said, "So what was that all about?"

May said, "I don't know, but you have been weaving in and out of lanes like Mario Andretti, and you are making me a nervous wreck. Now, after this prophet-of-doom call from Daniel, I'm even more nervous. I don't know what's up with him, but I am begging you to slow down. I'd rather get to Tenner Hall late and in one piece than not at all."

"OK. I'll slow down. I've made it to the front of the pack now anyhow. Those slow pokes were really frustrating me."

Perry didn't realize that his last strong effort to get stopped at their current traffic light, just before the Callow bridge, had, at the last moment, blown a serious hole in a corroded brake line. As he sat with his foot on the brake pedal, precious fluid was literally spraying out onto the street.

When the light turned green, he accelerated up onto the arched bridge like a race horse out of the gate. At the top he saw that their traffic light at the bottom of the bridge was red, and as they slalomed downward toward the busy, four-lane-by-six-lane intersection he applied the brakes. Suddenly fear gripped him.

"Oh no! The brakes are getting soft!" he yelled. Then he screamed, "No brakes! I have no brakes!"

Perry immediately kicked the brake pedal to the floor, but very little help came. After what seemed like an eternity (yet it was really only about a second of time) he pulled up the emergency brake lever, which brought some more help, but they were not going to stop in time. At that point, in his panic he thought only of somehow getting stopped. He was not yet thinking of the need to warn other drivers. Since they were indeed at the front of the pack, there were no other cars waiting ahead of them at the stoplight ahead. There was nothing between them and the cross-cutting traffic, which included all manner of cars, trucks, and big rigs traveling on a major thoroughfare located adjacent to that side of the river. At the last moment before they careened into the intersection, Perry finally thought to blow the horn. It did some good, but not enough.

As they entered the intersection, a gap allowed them to cross through most of the first lane of perpendicular traffic, but in the second lane, a large delivery truck skidded toward them with locked-up brakes. The truck slammed into their vehicle on the driver's side, killing Perry almost instantly. The angle of the truck and the force of the impact hurled their car into the far side of the intersection, against traffic headed the opposite way from the direction of the truck. A utility vehicle on that side had nowhere to go, and it struck them on the passenger side, severely injuring Tess, and fatally injuring May.

Their car was rolled over onto its top by the second impact, and it was then bumped two more times by other vehicles. Eventually they came to rest amidst discharged airbags, shattered glass, and torn, crumpled metal. May was still alive, but barely. They were hanging upside down in their seat belts. Tess's seat belt had probably saved her life, but now it was posing a problem. The location of her seat belt across her torso was a place of searing pain. She was bleeding from her head and several other places. Due to adrenaline, somehow Tess managed to free herself from the seat belt. She fell face-first onto the car roof beneath her. She reached forward through a small gap toward the front seats.

"Daddy?" she murmured desperately, "Mama?"

She heard nothing from her father, and only a faint groan from her mother.

"Mama? Mama! Are you all right? Daddy, are you all right?"

A blood-covered hand grasped hers, and her mother faintly whispered, "Daniel was right. I don't know how but he—"

"Mama? Mama! Mama!" Tess called, but there was no answer. Her mother had uttered her last words.

Through the pain, Tess wept before going into shock. Within minutes the blood loss rendered her unconscious.

Daniel had not ever departed for Tenner Hall. Due to what he felt God had impressed upon him, he sat at home, waiting. In the midst of desperation and a swirl of confusion, he prayed and tried to have faith. He flinched when the house phone rang. His mother answered. He could tell by her response that it was not good news. The caller was a girl from his high school, whose older sister had attended college with Tess. Thus the news of the accident made its way to Daniel. They quickly departed for the hospital.

Tess was already in emergency surgery when they arrived. Some of her internal organs had to be removed because they were damaged too badly to be saved. After over nine hours of intensive work, they were finally able to sew her up. The doctors were hopeful, yet could not promise that she would survive. Tess was severely swollen and heavily sedated, and she remained so for almost four days. Daniel visited the hospital often, and he was waiting at the hospital when Tess regained consciousness. By the time he was allowed in to visit her, she had been informed of her parents' deaths. She could not bring herself to appreciate his visit or his concern.

On the sixth day of her long hospitalization (the second day after she had regained consciousness) Daniel was allowed in to visit her not long after a doctor had left her room in the intensive care unit. The doctor had informed her of even more bad news.

Through clinched teeth she told Daniel, "I can never have kids. That's the latest news. Leave me alone, please."

With his head bowed, he obeyed her request. In utter desperation, he prayed for her on his way out. His prayer was interrupted by a lady in the main hall who seemed concerned and who looked like she was a relative of Tess. The lady spoke as though she knew him. She was dressed in white.

"Daniel, everything is going to be fine," she said. "Tess is going to be OK, and *one day she will be a mother*. Just trust God about everything."

Daniel nodded his head and asked, "Do I know you?"

"Yes!" she said, laughing. "Eventually you'll figure out how you know me."

Daniel scoured his memory, trying to remember if he had ever met her. He looked toward the doors of the intensive care unit and longed for a way to take away Tess's pain and despair. He felt completely helpless.

As he turned back toward the lady, Daniel said, "I know God can do miracles—"

He froze in mid-sentence because the woman was gone. It was as though she had disappeared into thin air.

Daniel felt like his mind was on overload. There was a nagging sense of urgency that caused frustration. It was as though something important was going on, yet he was missing it. He could not figure out what was the matter.

An ICU nurse that had seen them talking came around the corner. She walked up to Daniel and asked, "Was that lady a relative of Tess Addair, the patient in bed seven?"

"I'm not sure. I think so. Maybe," Daniel replied.

"Hmm," she observed, "I first saw that lady last week, the day Tess came in, right after they did her emergency surgery. It was odd though. I was just coming on duty. On my way in, I passed her. It looked as though she had just come out of the operating room area. That stuck in my mind because it was odd. Family and friends aren't allowed back there. The doctors do post-op counseling with the family in the waiting area. Also, she had on the exact same white suit that day. Was she in there with Tess?"

"Not that I know of," Daniel said. "She looks familiar, but I cannot remember where I've met her. She knew my name, and she said we know each other."

"Oh, OK," the employee sighed in relief. "She must be either a friend or a relative. No problem."

Daniel could not get the meeting out of his mind. The vanishing lady's words to him were burned into his memory.

Day after day Daniel returned to visit Tess. Visits were limited to 15 minutes in length. Day after day she ignored him. Sometimes she even asked him to leave. He always complied, but he always came back the next day. He knew in his heart that he loved Tess, yet he also knew that unless she came to God he could not pursue a relationship with her, let alone marry her. It would have been a sin before God to do so. He hoped she would come to God. However, she was in an emotional pit so deep that it seemed she might never escape. Tess was consumed with grief, despair, and emotional agony that hurt far worse than her physical wounds.

During one visit she said, "I am to live, but I am not a woman. Not only are my parents gone, but I am to be some miserable imitation of a woman who can never be a mother." Daniel knew that her only hope was God, and he knew that all he could do was pray. He tried to have faith as he pondered the words of the mysterious lady.

Tess was so harsh toward him that he did not dare to

raise the subject of God or salvation, let alone tell her about the strange lady and what she had spoken. After Tess was released from the hospital, Daniel did not feel welcome to visit her any further. Their friendship was on ice for the second time.

Daniel's pastor preached a sermon about how Christians should try to make up for their prior sins by repaying people to restore anything wrongfully taken from them. Daniel had obtained a job at a local sporting goods store, and when he got his first paycheck he decided to make some things right. The following week he walked into a grocery store from which he, as a child, had stolen some candy and a toy several years earlier. He laid some money down on the counter at the service desk and told an employee that he needed to speak to the manager. He waited wordlessly until the store's owner finally came to the service desk. One would have thought Daniel was green and had four heads from the way they stared at him while he explained to the store owner why he was there.

Daniel completed his statements by saying, "Here is money to repay what I stole as a child, and I would certainly understand if you need to call the police and press charges."

The store owner finally smiled and said, "In all my years of fighting shrinkage at the hands of shoplifters,

I've been cussed, fought, attacked, spit at, run from—you name it. I have never, ever seen anyone come back to repay our store. You, son, are a first. We won't be pressing charges. If you ever need a job, you come here and work for me."

Daniel's next two stops were the homes of two of his cousins in Forrest Dell, about six and a half hours away. He called first to arrange a day when he could visit. He handled the smaller transgression first. He sat down with his cousin, Christi, from whom he had stolen about $17 in cash (back when she still lived at home with her parents). Daniel gave her a $50 bill and explained what he had done, and how young he had been when he did it.

She shook her head and said, "You thieving brat. Thank you for making this right. I suspected, but I never had proof. What made you confess? How did you learn your lesson?"

He explained that it was not that he ever got caught or suffered punishment, but rather he had been saved and touched by God. She was not especially interested after that part of the conversation, but she thanked him for the repayment.

Finally, it was time to talk to Rick, the cousin from whom he had stolen the ring. He brought with him the ring and all the cash he had remaining, about $160.

"Dan the man!" his cousin said when he opened his front door to Daniel.

Daniel sat down with him, brought out the ring, and explained everything. When Rick finally comprehended what was happening, he grew angry.

Rick yelled, "You really messed me up back then, cuz! A guy I knew had paid $1,400 for that ring new, but he got in a jam and sold it to me for $700. I was buying it then for my girlfriend so I could ask her to marry me. It had taken me months to save up that money! When you stole the ring from me, it set me back. That girl was really pretty, and she really wanted to get married. While I was pulling my hair out looking for the ring, another guy who had money swooped in, offered her a nice ring, and took her away from me. She married that guy. I was miserable for months over that! I ought to punch you good, man! I ought to beat you down!"

Daniel repeatedly explained how sorry he was. After a couple of minutes Rick calmed down. Daniel offered to either repay him a full $1,400 (over a few months' time) or else give him the ring back.

Rick demurely said, "Man, you don't have to pay me back, and I don't need the ring now. I'm happily married to a different woman. Look, I appreciate you coming over here to confess and offering to make this right."

Daniel insisted, "I want to make this right. I need to. I want you to take this cash, and I will be mailing you checks for the next several months, OK?"

Rick agreed, and Daniel made his way back home.

Over the course of the next few months, he sent money to Rick, eventually paying him $1,400. Daniel then owned the ring. Yet he did not have the girl.

Perry and May Addair had perished without any last will and testament in place, but they had something much better, called a revocable living trust. Their lawyer friend, Roy, was rare among attorneys because he had studied estate planning. Thus he knew how to write a living trust well, and, more importantly, he knew why having one was so helpful. He always advised what was best for his clients, not what would pad the pockets of attorneys. Although he received significantly less money for writing a living trust than he could make from a probate case resulting from a will, the trust was by far the better option for all the families he served.

This was true for many reasons. Their state law decreed that any and all assets owned by the deceased had to go before the court in a probate process that was both maddeningly slow and fraught with fees. There were court costs, attorney fees (ranging from 4% to 10% of the total value of the estate), and appraisal fees, just to name a few. Furthermore, once an estate went before a court, the judge was empowered to actually change the will of the deceased or even throw it out and start from scratch. About one-third of the time, judges did change the will of the deceased in some way. Also, when issues of oversight and guardianship were left up to the courts, often the appointments made were the least beneficial as far as anyone except attorneys were concerned. (Some attorneys were friends with the judges, and so the courts were prone to award estate oversight and guardianship—and thus the resulting exorbitant fee income as well—to those friends instead of to loving relatives of surviving family members.)

Early in their marriage, Perry and May had taken action based on their lawyer's good advice. They had Roy draw up the papers to create their living trust. Then they took the vital steps to "fund" the trust. They had their home deeded in the name of the trust and their cars titled in the name of the trust. Their insurance policies were set so that any claims would be paid to the trust with Tess as the contingent beneficiary of the trust.

During the process, Roy posed key questions of them about guardianship, so that he could include all the stipulations needed to fulfill their wishes. Their documents specified that if both of them were to ever die or become incompetent or incapacitated, Perry's brother and sister-in-law, Percy and Melinda, would become the legal guardians of Tess until she turned eighteen. Also, in such a case, Percy was to oversee the trust on Tess's behalf until she came of age.

Because Perry and May had wisely taken these steps, after their deaths there was no chance for the courts to get involved with Tess's guardianship. Also, because they did not own any assets in their own names, there was nothing to go before a probate court. There was no way that an attorney could be granted oversight.

When Tess was released from the hospital, she went to stay with her Aunt Melinda and Uncle Percy. Tess's childhood home (and the other assets) remained in trust for her until it could legally become hers. This included their one remaining vehicle, which was a Jeep. (The sedan was totaled in the accident.)

Tess slowly recovered. She met regularly with both a physiotherapist and a psychiatrist. After several months she moved back home and returned to classes to pursue a postgraduate degree. She was living on insurance money that was channeled through the trust fund, and she also had scholarships and grants for her schooling. The state-assigned social worker was satisfied that she was recovering and living well, and that things were stabilizing for her.

A man in some of her classes, named Mitchell, took an interest in her. He began to talk to her, and he started asking her out on dates. She brushed him off, but he kept on coming back for more rejection. Eventually she agreed to one date, during which she planned to explain things, which, she felt sure, would put an end to his pursuit. She met him after class at a nearby restaurant. After a minute of small talk she coldly stated the facts.

"Mitch, I appreciate your interest in me, but you

should know that both my parents were killed in a terrible car accident, and I am angry at God and at the world. I am not interested in a relationship, and furthermore, I am damaged goods—"

At that point he interrupted her by saying, "Look we all have done things in past relationships that we're not proud of. I won't hold that against you if you won't hold it against me."

Tess recalculated, and then she continued, "Thank you for sharing that. I was not talking about lost virginity. I am still a virgin. The fact that you are not does not help you in pursuit of me. I was talking about the fact that I can never have children. I was severely injured in the wreck. Some of my internal organs were damaged. I am not whole. I am likely to have hormonal imbalances. I am likely to have a difficult time desiring a man physically, and I am likely to suffer depression over my inability to ever become a mother. In short, being married to me would likely be a nightmare. I came here tonight to give you the fairness of explaining this up front: It's really not you. It's me. That's not just a line. It's the truth."

"OK. Message received loud and clear," Mitchell said, and then he added, "but, hey, who wants kids anyway? Not me. Little brats. Who needs them? Are you sure there is no way I can get you to reconsider?"

"Not now," Tess fired back. "I don't know if there is a man I want, but I will say this. I don't want someone who does not like kids. I might want someone who wants kids, yet would love me enough to do without them. I think I will go home now."

At that, she left. They had not even ordered yet.

When she got home, she grabbed the junk mail and bills from the mailbox, and some common neighborhood handouts from the screen door. As usual, her home got its fair share of the stuff. There were sometimes handbills from this church or that one, or from one group or another, or information about some fundraiser for this or that.

One paper had already left her hand and made it to the trash can when she noticed the name "Rev. Daniel Talbot" on it. She fished it out and saw that Daniel's church was having a series of special services at which Daniel was to be the special speaker. His picture was shown beneath the fold, proving there was no mistake. Out loud she slowly said to herself, "Daniel—my Daniel —is a preacher. I can't believe it."

For a moment, she wondered if her home had been singled out for this flier. She went out on the front porch and looked around the neighborhood. Over half the other homes still had their copy of the canary yellow flier either on their front porch or on the gate of their fence. She envisioned teens from Daniel's church passing down her street, knocking on her door while she was in class, or perhaps while she was at the restaurant giving Mitchell the facts.

She went back inside and dragged a carton of ice cream out of the freezer like an alcoholic reaches for his wine. She sat on the couch and pondered details she had not let herself remember for months. She thought about Daniel—her sweet Daniel—and how she had rejected him, and yet he kept coming back. With sorrow and regret, she thought about how harshly she had treated him, even though obviously he was the real deal and apparently had a hardline connection straight to God. She berated herself for how she had bitterly chased him away until he eventually stopped coming around anymore. Her tears dripped into her ice cream as she longed to hear his voice. She wept. She polished off the carton of ice cream, and then she curled up on the couch and cried herself to sleep.

The first night of the revival, Daniel was naturally nervous. He had preached at his home church several times, but never in a special revival service. *There's a first time for everything,* he thought. In the minutes before the start of the service, many of the church's members were gathered at the front of the sanctuary, seeking God's face in fervent prayer. Daniel was there as well, on his face, prostrate on the carpet, praying for God's anointing. Suddenly someone firmly tapped him on the shoulder. He looked up to see a friend pointing toward the main entrance.

Tess was standing in the foyer. A wave of emotion overwhelmed Daniel. His tears flowed like a river. He made his way to the foyer where an usher was greeting her. She was as beautiful as ever. She smiled at him, and then cast her eyes down, hoping he would not be angry with her. As he drew near, she could see that he had been crying.

"Tess, it's so good to see you here. I never dreamed I'd see you tonight."

"Daniel, I'm so sorry for how I've mistreated you. I'm a broken person. If I have any hope of healing, it's either in you or in God or both. I don't know where things are going. I just know I need help."

"Tess, God loves you, and so do I. Everything is going to be just fine."

Tess caught the 'so do I' part that Daniel had said. It was not as strong as a flat out 'I love you,' but it was too deliberate to have been just a slip of the tongue. She was caught off guard by Daniel even *implying* that he loved her.

"You love me?" she asked in surprise.

Without any hesitation Daniel answered, "Yes."

Tess looked down at the floor and asked, "Are we talking about the platonic love of a Christian for a lost soul, or something more?"

"Both," said Daniel, "but I cannot pursue *that* kind of relationship with you unless you turn to God. I was kinda hoping that was why you came here tonight."

Without looking up she asked, "But what about the fact that I can never have children?"

"I would love to be a daddy," Daniel assured her. "I want that more than almost anything, but I love you more." (He still did not mention that a mysterious lady had told him that Tess would be a mother someday, because he had no idea how Tess might take that.)

Tess thought, *That was not just a hint. It was a flat out 'I love you.' He said it.* She finally lifted her eyes, and her tears welled up and overflowed.

"I don't feel very lovable," she finally said.

Daniel tried to come up with something profound to say. He considered all she had been through and how long it would take her to recover. He wanted to find some way to tell her that how she felt right at that moment was not permanent, or at least it did not have to be; he had faith that she would be whole again. Yet he somehow sensed that there was no way to phrase it without trivializing her loss. He did not want to marginalize her heartbreaking circumstances and the trauma she had endured. Finally he settled for simply trying to convince her that his love was unfeigned.

"Well, it's true," he said. "I do."

Tess knew that the unwritten rules about relationships stipulated in all capital letters that in an instance such as this she was supposed to reciprocate by telling him that she loved him, too. However, she could not bring herself to say it. It may have been because the only people she had ever truly loved with all her heart had been taken from her. Perhaps she had a subconscious fear that letting herself love Daniel would lead to him being taken away as well.

Daniel had a strong impulse to hug her right there in the foyer, in front of God and everyone, but he knew that would have raised some eyebrows in the church.

He suddenly remembered where they were and said, "Umm, I guess we should go on in."

"Right."

Tess was not yet ready to run to the altar and turn her life over to God, but she was finally open to hearing the truth. She could not get around the fact that somehow Daniel had knowledge from God, in advance, that they should not have attempted to travel to the commencement ceremonies that day. She did not understand the Bible, or God, and she did not know what to do, except she was pretty certain that listening to Daniel was a wise thing to do.

As the church service progressed, Tess strongly sensed a Presence, which she somehow knew was the Spirit of the Lord. The sense of Him was thick and palpable in the room that night, especially while the church people were singing and making gestures of praise to God. Tess was startled by how strong her perception of this Presence was. This could *not* be ignored. She then clearly understood why people called His Spirit *holy*. She also finally grasped why some of the people got so excited in their praise gestures. She was only vaguely aware of the meaning of the word holy, yet she knew that without a doubt the Presence in the room that night was powerful, utterly sweet, and *holy* if ever that word was rightly deserved in its use.

She felt the same Presence again during the time in the service when Daniel preached a message entitled "From Problem to Portal" using Exodus 14:14-31. He showed how that what seemed like a problem was turned into a portal by the Lord God when, by the hand of Moses, He parted the sea so the Israelites could escape from the pursuing armies of Pharaoh, passing over the seabed on dry ground, with a wall of water on the left hand and on the right. Not only did God make the sea a portal, but He made it a filter as well. For although the Israelites could pass through it, the Egyptians could not. When the Egyptians tried to pass through the sea while chasing the Israelites, the waters of the sea returned to normal, overthrowing the oppressor's soldiers, chariots, and horsemen, drowning them all. Daniel preached that God is able to take our problems and use them as a portal to bring us to a better place. He can also use that same portal as a filter to prevent any oppressor from following us.

It was just a simple message, but it was made powerful that night by the added touch of God's anointing and because of the truth it conveyed. When Tess felt that Presence dripping off Daniel's words, it made her feel endeared to him more than ever. It made her want to accept Daniel's words and his faith. The touch of that Presence made her want to become a believer. She was not one to ever leap into something without careful consideration, so she refrained from showing how she felt. For the time being she tried to hide her inward desire to make the kind of change in her life that Daniel had told her about long before, back when she was only 12 years old.

Top, right of center (third from left): Aldyn Prayer Tower.
Top, left (shrouded in fog): The sixth Place of Meeting.

Chapter III

Sset

At this point, we must divert our attention away from Tess and Daniel, and learn something of a world called Sset. The Ssettian creatures are a brilliant and colorful display of God's limitless creativity. Among the most fascinating are the Corlan, a kind that is significantly human-like. The Corlan are the crowning glory of their world, just as humans are the crowning glory of this one; essentially they are our counterpart. Like humans, they were made in the image of God.

The Corlan are a noble, righteous people that share many similarities with us (by the deliberate choice of the Creator of both worlds), yet their species also has some interesting distinctions. Some of the differences include: The Corlan have never committed any sin of rebellion that would warrant a universal curse. Therefore the very first Corlan is still alive. They have never lost a single baby. They do not abort their young. No Corlan has ever murdered another. No Corlan has ever died. Their world has no sickness or death.

Furthermore, the Corlan have a triple-redundant memory storage system, part of which is a regular function of their brains, and part of which is an aspect of their world's ecosystem. Regarding their memory system (as well as their reproduction process, which is somewhat different from ours), some of what goes on within their brains, as well as the part that happens outside of their bodies, is due to a vast fleet of powerful microbes living in symbiotic harmony with the Corlan. This microbiotic substance (unique to their beautiful world) would probably be described by humans as *bacteria* (albeit helpful, not harmful). The first Corlan named it *surati*—an "engineering marvel" that reveals the glory of God.

The reader may already be aware that each and every living cell (both of a human body and of other creatures) contains many *extremely small* protein machines that do crucial tasks at a molecular level. These protein machines are essential for life because the jobs they do are necessary for physical life as we know it. Think of these machines as God's own type of nanotechnology—protein nanites that He designed and implemented in all of us. Similarly, the cells of these Ssettian microbes contain tiny machines that not only do the kinds of jobs that we know get done inside living cells, but also they do some pretty amazing things regarding the memories of each Corlan family. Mind you, the microbes themselves are like "machines" too, but they do electro-chemical work in the Corlan brains, not molecular work. As tiny as the microbes are, they are not nearly tiny enough to do work at the molecular scale. These protein nanites are *inside* the cells of the microbes. The nanites are so small they make the microbes seem gigantic.

Because of the cooperation of these surati microbes, the Corlan are blessed with what humans might call "genetic memory." (Although that phrase is not an entirely accurate way to describe the process, it will do until we can explain further.) Each Corlan eventually has access to all of the memories that its particular ancestors (of the same gender) had accumulated prior to the various moments of reproduction in that family's history that repeatedly split the internal memory chain in a given ancestor and then added it into the ongoing memory chain handed down across succeeding generations.

The reader does not need to bother with understanding any of this, as there will not be any quiz on it, but the Corlan memory stream is expressed (transferred) to their young in a manner somewhat like this:

Individual Corlan have a multi-tier memory process. The first and second tiers work like our own—their short-term and near-term memory (which is an electrical process that is based on neurons firing, just as in humans) is selectively written into long-term memory (which is a process that is chemically aided, just as in humans). Chemical actuators (such as adrenalin) serve as a kind of glue to cause the long-term memories to "stick" (just like what happens in our minds).

That is where the memory similarities cease. Although their brains are remarkably similar to ours, the presence of the surati causes a striking difference. The Ssettian microbes can live quite well outside of the Corlan (and some of them temporarily do so following each Corlan reproduction cycle), but they are designed to make their home inside the Corlan brain. The surati multiply as needed and distribute themselves within their host's brain matter. For all practical intents and purposes, the collective surati "substance" becomes an additional type of brain matter for the host, interfacing with his or her long-term memory regions.

Thus each Corlan brain possesses an additional electro-chemical factory as well as a distributed network of biological memory storage devices comprised of the vast array of molecular nanites within the microbes.

Each night, while a Corlan is asleep, the microbes work diligently translating that day's new long-term memories for their internal protein machines, which then work diligently encoding those memories into strands of what we might call "memory deoxyribonucleic acid" (we'll call it M-DNA for short). This biological storage medium, which can hold massive amounts of information, is used to store memories at the molecular level. It was designed just for this purpose. Eventually those same memories are available to be transmitted to that Corlan's offspring in M-DNA format.

Those same protein machines also work during the night to decode the prior memories of all the ancestors (of the same gender) of that sleeping Corlan, and then the nanites manufacture the needed chemicals and guide the microbes in retranslating the memories into electro-chemically stored information in the Corlan's long-term memory. The transferred data (the memory record of a given Corlan's family) comes from the portions of M-DNA strands that were built inside the parent, grand-parent, and great-grandparent, etc., prior to the new-born's existence, which were then made available to the new baby's brain in a parental ritual following his or her birth. Previous events, technical knowledge, thoughts, and emotions are all preserved and transferred.

A new Corlan is not aware of these prior memories at birth or for some time afterward. The Corlan are unable to simply discern memories straight from the M-DNA alone. They can only recall the past memories once the information has been decoded from the M-DNA and retranslated into the chemically based storage medium (the same kind of system from which the memories originated). Thus the Corlan slowly gain awareness of their collective memory during their maturing process. Each night while a young Corlan sleeps, he or she gets additional long-term memories. Each morning when he or she awakes, the young Corlan has all day to ponder these new memories while at play and/or at work.

The Corlan do have schools, but their purpose for such an enterprise is based on entirely different needs. Their schools are simply a place where new knowledge is "manually" shared across the various familial memory streams present within their kind.

Having these ongoing chains of memories means that each Corlan *naturally* understands the wisdom of obeying God, and each knows the benefits that obedience brings. Also, each one remembers *firsthand* the Lord's words spoken directly to the very first Corlan, a couple whose name is Shao.

The Corlan home world, called Sset, is a planet-sized moon (about 1.12 *earth mass* in size) with its own rather intricate atmosphere. Sset is a distant satellite of a gas giant. (A *gas giant* is a huge planet consisting mostly of gaseous elements. Jupiter is the largest of multiple gas giants within our own star system.) The Corlan named their gas giant T'and (rhymes with *hand*). T'and orbits a star they named P'av (rhymes with *have*). Their star is a nice, bright, hot one. Our scientists would call it a G-type, main sequence star. P'av is part of a galaxy called H'aro (which rhymes with *arrow*). Their galaxy is located in an alternate universe (a space-time that is disconnected from our own) that the Corlan call Cyntu. (We should mention that *cyntu* is also their regular word for any given universe, so the word is both a general noun and a proper name. Because of the memories handed down from their eldest couple, they are aware of our separate space-time, and they perceive it as 'another' cyntu.)

If it seems strange to our reader that the people of that world would call their universe and our own by the same name, please consider that we would do the same. We speak of "the universe" when referring to our own, and of "other universes" when pondering whether such exist. The word *universe* is a proper name, and yet in a way it is not.

Their cyntu, or universe, has some fundamental differences from ours, of which at least two are very noteworthy: (1) their time flows at a rate that is ever so slightly faster than ours (at a ratio of about 1 : 0.968241), and (2) their universe has a crucial difference in how its gravity works. From our point of view, it is what we might call a gravitational "glitch."

At a certain altitude from any mass (proportionately distanced from that mass, and manifested in all directions), gravity suddenly pushes (instead of pulling). Elsewhere (higher and lower) all is as we would expect. At lower altitudes (nearer than that certain distance) gravity pulls. At higher altitudes (beyond that certain distance) gravity returns to pulling again (as we would consider normal). Yet at that certain altitude, in all directions, their gravity pushes away from the mass instead of pulling toward it.

This results in a gravity "trap" that is particularly noticeable around the stars and planets of that universe. Stars there will virtually always be surrounded by a sphere of debris and energy. A host star's gravity trap holds asteroids, dust, interstellar gases, and other physical elements, as well as some of the emissions from the star itself (much of which gets bounced by the debris before eventually being absorbed by it). These elements all come together to form a highly charged, volatile sphere around the star. Bounced energy inside the sphere causes it to be very hot internally.

The Corlan word for such a sphere is *sedondi*, which we might translate for our readers as *outsphere*. For the Corlan, the same word applies to a planet's outsphere as well as to a star's. However, depending on a host planet's location, planetary outspheres may be more volatile or less volatile, and they may or may not carry a lot of energy or significant charge. Sset itself does not have much of an outsphere, for a variety of reasons. As a smaller body, its gravity trap is rather weak, and Sset is secluded by being inside the T'andian outsphere.

Each such debris field (whether stellar or planetary) is usually only a partial sphere, because outspheres often have holes or gaps at their top and bottom, located above the axial poles of the host star or host planet. An outsphere is not just a ring—not just a flat disc such as we are familiar with in our universe. Our type of planetary ring exists only within a limited plane that is always perpendicular to the axis of its host mass (think of the rings of Saturn in our solar system). In that universe, an outsphere extends upwards and downwards away from such a limited plane, in a way that a ring cannot.

In the case of a star's outsphere, the debris field can intercept and diffuse a lot of the star's light, and therefore absorb a lot of the star's energy. This gas giant, T'and, was perfectly placed by God in such a way that part of its outsphere intersects with its star's outsphere (actually interrupting it). If the gas giant had been located too far into its star's outsphere, life would be impossible on Sset because the trapped energy from P'av (their star) would bake their world to a crisp. By the same token, if the gas giant was placed too far away (outside the star's outsphere), life would be impossible on Sset because it would be far too cold.

As it is, God in His marvelous wisdom granted them a paradise. T'and's outsphere is, of course, in motion as its contents continually orbit around the gas giant. At all times, a certain percentage of the huge planet's outsphere is peaking inside the star's outsphere. As soon as the debris (in its orbital journey around T'and) peaks into P'av's outsphere and becomes directly exposed to the star's full energy output (as well as becoming a conduit of the trapped energy of the star's outsphere), that portion of T'and's outsphere quickly absorbs so much energy that it literally glows. The longer it stays within the star's outsphere, the hotter it gets and the brighter it glows. A great deal of energy gets transferred to portions of the outsphere debris above and below (into portions that do not even make it into the P'avian outsphere).

Even after that highly energized section of debris departs from the star's outsphere, it continues to glow for a major portion of its quick journey around its gas giant host. Meanwhile, trailing portions of T'and's outsphere (that have already made the whole trip and have grown cooler and somewhat dim) are continually brought around for another pass, as once again they enter the star's outsphere. Thus, a perennially glowing strip is always present in the sky above almost all portions of Sset. The width of that glowing strip spans about one fourth of the massive height of the gas giant's outsphere. The portion of the glowing strip closest to P'av is always the hottest, and the Ssettian primary spring is when their moon world is located on that side of T'and, nearest to P'av. Their secondary spring is while they have recently passed near to P'av, as their moon world moves further around T'and. Sset also has two fall seasons. Their first fall is when they are on the far side of T'and, opposite of the direction of their star. The gas giant then eclipses the brightest side of the glow strip, but there is still much warmth in the fading glow strip above them on that far side. The secondary fall comes after that, when they move out of the gas giant's shadow. During that period, the portion of the glow strip directly above them is becoming its coolest and dimmest, but they are within a line of sight to the warmest portion of the glow strip, and they begin to be warmed additionally by it from a distance as they are getting ready for the primary spring again.

The time it takes for a portion of T'and's outsphere located at its equator to make a full orbit around the gas giant is very short; only about 94 of Sset's rotational days. However, Sset and all her sister moons orbit the gas giant much more slowly. A full orbit of Sset around T'and takes about ten earth years (not accounting for the time rate differential between the two universes). That full journey around the gas giant is how they mark their year. (Their word for that period of time is *cam*.)

In their calendar, they pay absolutely no attention to how long it takes T'and to orbit P'av. This is because the host star's energy is so evenly distributed within its outsphere, and the gas giant's orbital path around the star is so perfectly circular. (Its closest point, which we call perihelion, and its farthest point, which we call aphelion, are practically the same distance.) Thus T'and's orbit around P'av causes very minimal effect on their weather and ecosystem.

Of the 28 other satellites (moons) of T'and, most are smaller than Sset. The moons all form an orbital pattern of concentric circles at various altitudes. Some are farther away from T'and than Sset, while others are nearer. Sset also has a nicely sized moon of its own—a satellite of a satellite. They named their moon T'el.

There are occasional light shows in the Ssettian sky just about any time of their year except during their first fall season. The colorful bursts are caused by common interactions between P'av's outsphere and T'and's outsphere. However, as beautiful as those displays are, they don't hold a candle to the magnificent light show that happens whenever some of the moons in the outer orbits vertically align with each other near the hottest point of the glow strip. This event, called *C'alimnet*, regularly occurs once every twelfth cam. It lasts for many days. (C'alimnet is also the name of T'and's outermost moon, whose 12-cam orbital cycle is the primary factor in the timing of the alignments. Regarding which other moons are involved, the event's other participants can vary.)

When the moons align, they form a path of targets for massive stellar energy arcs originating from the hottest areas of the glow strip. During the alignments, huge amounts of energy are conducted through the atmosphere that clings to the inner surface of the outsphere and on through the trace gases that drift around at altitudes ranging down to where the outermost moons reside, causing an effect to which nothing here compares. As the participating moons are engulfed in the amber glow of charged plasma particles, their own atmospheres light up as well. (An artist's rendition of a C'alimnet event's display is depicted on the cover of this book.) The Corlan always find the event to be breathtaking. They look forward to it, and they have a huge C'alimnet festival to coincide with the event, during which they celebrate God's goodness to them in a huge way.

Previously we mentioned the Corlan word for outsphere. The concept of *sedondi* is fundamental to the Corlan's only language. For example, consider these Corlan words:

- *trasedondi* - literally translated as "glow of the [out]sphere" or "light from the [out]sphere";
- *telsedondi* - means "darkness of the [out]sphere."

Similarly, fellowship with other Corlan can initiate friends into one's personal sedondi. The result is:

- *issesedondi* - means "one within my [out]sphere." Issesedondi is the Corlan word for friend or friendship.

Likewise, anything that undermines, hinders, or prevents friendship is called:

- *ettosedondi* - "that which opposes my [out]sphere [-and/or threatens what lies within]."

  Ettosedondi is their word for enemy.

Since no Corlan has ever truly been a full-blown enemy in the vicious sense of some human enemies here, the reader might fairly wonder why they even have such a word in their language. The reason is this: God's words to them prophesied a terrible Ettosedondi to come; a truly malicious Corlan whose rise was foreseen by God.

CHAPTER IV

Wisdom

When the church service was concluded, Daniel invited Tess to join him and several other church members for a snack and some fellowship. She agreed, and she was pleasantly surprised to see how much fun the people had—good, clean fun—and how grounded, humble, and intelligent they were. Tess could tell that this was not some bunch of ignorant hicks who had been duped into thinking they needed a crutch of religion, and they were not some miserable group of people who hated the shackles of religion yet felt compelled to suffer anyhow.

One of the men was a doctor. Another was an engineer. One of the ladies was a business owner. Even those members who seemed the poorest were level-headed people who had a great sense of fulfillment and genuinely enjoyed their lives.

There was a lively conversation going on at the next table about scientific reasons to believe in the Creator. The pastor and the doctor were involved, as well as a family that Tess took to be some of the poorest people in the room, and yet they all spoke as equals. Tess watched and listened. It took only a few moments of hearing Pastor Blaylock speak for Tess to discern that he was a well-studied, brilliant man who had dedicated years of his life to answering the very kinds of questions that Tess wanted to ask.

That collection of moments caused something to happen in Tess. The realization dawned on her that while she was probably lightyears ahead of all these people in areas such as chemistry, physics, and quantum mechanics, she was lightyears behind them with regard to spiritual development. She had just met Someone that very night —the true God whose existence she could not deny— and yet most of them had already known Him for many years. They had a long-term relationship with this powerful Being that she had never even met until then.

For the first time in her life, Tess was shy, at a loss for words. Her normal level of confidence, which had allowed her to speak fearlessly in university lecture halls and college research labs, was gone. She began second-guessing herself on every question she desired to ask, and in the end she asked nothing, but rather just sat, listening and learning.

Daniel offered to follow Tess home, to make sure she made it safely, but she declined, saying she would be fine. She left the radio off (which was unusual for her) and drove home in silence.

Later, as she sat alone in the living room of her empty house, Tess squarely faced her critical decision. She sensed the ultra-importance of this crossroads in her life. Would she use carnal logic to scrutinize, criticize, undermine, and extinguish the spark of faith that God had given her that night at Daniel's church? Or would she use His gift of faith to overcome her fallen nature? She had suddenly become very aware of the sin curse within her. Would she choose worldly wisdom or the spiritual wisdom from above?

Her lower nature raised what seemed like a thousand objections, including a lot of so-called "scientific" oppositions. Yet she could not deny that Daniel had displayed a miraculous knowledge of the future, and she did not want to deny the Presence that she had felt while she sat in their church sanctuary during the worship and singing and again while Daniel preached.

At exactly 2:47 AM, Tess made her choice. She made the right decision. She chose God, salvation, and Daniel. As she drifted off to sleep afterward, she had hope in her heart for the first time since before the accident.

Although this time the hope was stronger than any she had ever known before.

The next day she called Daniel.

"Hello?" Daniel answered.

"Helloooo!" she practically sang. The sound of his voice was like music to her.

"Well, you sound chipper!" Daniel exclaimed.

"Daniel, there is no sense beating around the bush," she said. "Even though I don't understand everything, and even though I cannot figure any of this out on my own, and even though I have a thousand questions, I have decided to follow God. I believe. I believe in Him, and I believe in you. I need you to help me know what to do. Where do we go from here?"

"Tess, that's awesome! You should come and talk to Pastor Blaylock, and we need to get you scheduled to be water baptized. Also, you need to approach God directly in asking Him to fill you with His Spirit. That experience can happen for you at any time and at any place. If you pray for that now, He could fill you right now."

At that, Tess suddenly felt more nervous than she had ever been. She became acutely aware of her faults, flaws, inadequacies, doubts, and fears. Every bit of harshness that she had heaped onto Daniel suddenly weighed on her like a truckload of lead.

"Daniel," she said, "I suddenly feel overwhelmingly... dirty. All I can think about is how wrong I have been and how unworthy I am." After a pause she added, "I guess I am becoming aware that I am a sinner. I truly understand what you meant about being a slave to sin."

"That's all right," Daniel offered. "Just remember that God's gift of salvation and His gift of His Spirit to you are exactly that: gifts. These are not based on your worthiness. They are based on the worthiness of the Lord Jesus, paid for by His blood through His sinless death on the cross. Just pray and call on the name of Jesus. He will come and help you. He will come and save you."

With a nod of affirmation Tess said, "Daniel, I count this as the most important decision I will ever make. Everything else pales in comparison to the significance of this. If you think we can meet the pastor today, then I am not going to my classes today."

"I will call him and call you right back," Daniel promised.

He did, and a meeting was set for 2:00 that afternoon. Tess drove to the church, where she parked beside Daniel's car. Right on time, she went in to find them talking in the foyer while waiting for her. She smiled and shrugged her shoulders in nervous anticipation of—she knew not what.

Pastor Blaylock led them both into his study office, where they entered into a time of Bible study and conversation. The pastor showed her things from the Scriptures that made perfect sense to her. Some of it amazed her. Finally, he encouraged her to obey all that they had read and discussed. As they all bowed their heads to pray, she spoke to God directly, out loud, in honest repentance and in a sincere request for His Spirit to be given to her. She was shocked and filled with wonder when He answered her immediately.

Although apparently her body did not move anywhere, He carried her away somehow. From some distance, she heard a woman's voice saying beautiful things in an ancient-sounding language that was completely unknown to her. As she enjoyed the same Presence that she had felt the night before, she listened intently to the woman's voice saying words so exquisite that she wished it would never end. She lost all track of time. At some point, she began to realize the voice she was hearing was her own. She suddenly found herself back in her body, in the chair in the pastor's study. Her mouth was saying those exquisite words in that ancient-sounding tongue. Her eyes had been closed the whole time. All at once, she stopped speaking, opened her eyes widely, and looked at Daniel, then at the pastor, and back again. As they smiled with giddy excitement and shouted praises to the Lord, Tess finally thought to shut her mouth, which had been hanging open in amazement. Her tears began to flow as the full impact of the experience hit her. She had been filled with the Spirit of the Creator of the universe.

"How long—?" she stammered.

"Almost half an hour," Daniel said, showing her the clock on his cell phone.

"You gotta be kidding me," she said. It had seemed like 30 seconds or a minute.

With a solemn sense of marking the occasion, the pastor declared, "Tess, the 'old you' is now dead. The 'old you' has been crucified with Christ. What we must do now, is bury the 'old you' in a watery grave. Through water baptism in Jesus name, the 'old you' goes into the tomb with Jesus, and the 'new you' comes out of the water, just as Jesus came out of the tomb. Are you ready to be baptized now?"

"Yes!" she declared.

The pastor's wife had come in by that time, along with two other church sisters, one of whom was Daniel's mother. They were all teary eyed as they heard what had happened. They guided Tess to the changing room where she donned a baptismal robe, and then they led her back to a special area where the church's baptistery was located.

The entire series of events became seared into her memory. The pastor had everyone pray, and he encouraged Tess to call upon the name of the Lord.

"Jesus!" she shouted. It was the only way she could think of to obey the pastor's words. Everyone had their hands lifted, so she lifted hers as well.

"Jesus!" she shouted again.

Then the pastor had her to hold her nose while he spoke a few words about her being identified with the Lord's death, burial, and resurrection as she had repented, been filled with the Spirit, and was being baptized in the name of the Lord Jesus Christ, and he swiftly shifted her weight back and took her down into the water. That same beautiful, ancient-sounding language came to her again as she came up from the water. As she began to say the God-given words, she again lost all track of time.

Later, many of the church members gathered for the second night in the series of revival services. The people all called her "Sister Tess." Although it struck her as odd, she liked it. As they all rejoiced over what God had done for her, Tess broke down in tears again. She knew that she had gone from being alone to having a whole church as her spiritual family.

CHAPTER V

Tess

Daniel finally felt the liberty to tell Tess about the mysterious woman at the hospital and the encouraging (if perplexing) words that she had spoken to him.

At first Tess just laughed and said, "That would be some miracle! I no longer have all the body parts to make that happen!" However, after she had responded in that way she felt badly about it, and so she added, "I believe God really can do miracles, and I sure would love it if He somehow found a way for that to come true."

"He can," Daniel said.

Tess asked, "Do you think it was for real? Do you think God plans to do that somehow? If not, it would be a pretty cruel joke to play on someone."

Daniel said, "I believe it. I don't know how or when, but I believe God will do that somehow, someday."

Some time later Tess said, "I wish you had felt free to tell me about that lady earlier, but I know I was treating you so harshly that I made it impossible."

Daniel just smiled at her. He did not speak, but the way he held her hand conveyed volumes.

Once Tess finally turned to God, it cleared the way for Daniel to be able to pursue a romantic relationship with her. He had loved her for longer than he could remember, and Tess knew that she felt the same way about him. Daniel had previously counseled privately with Pastor Blaylock about his ongoing situation with Tess, and the pastor had an accurate sense of how the two felt about each other.

As Daniel and Tess formally entered a dating relationship (and before either one had mentioned marriage), Pastor Blaylock counseled them both that perpetual dating and long engagements were used by worldly people who did not know how to discern the will of God through prayer, and who also did not mind one bit sinning against God by fornicating during their dating or engagement. He advised them to go straight to God, get an answer, trust the Lord, and act on that answer.

He suggested that they take a week or two off from their relationship, during which time they should each pray separately, and fast, to seek God for an answer as to whether or not they were right for each other, in God's eyes. If the Lord's answer turned out to be yes, then he advised them to set a date and get married. If the Lord's answer was no, he advised them to not date as it would just set them up for heartache, pain, and needless temptation.

Daniel had already been praying and fasting for that very answer for months, and inwardly he felt that he already had a green light from God. Nevertheless, for Tess's benefit he indicated he was willing to do what the pastor suggested. Tess agreed.

For two weeks they did not date or call one another. They saw each other only at church. Whenever Tess prayed about it, she felt a peace from the Lord, and the thought of Daniel was always accompanied by a pleasant touch of the Lord's anointing. She took this to mean the Lord was clearly saying yes. (She was correct.)

As they approached the Sunday at the two-week mark, Tess trusted and hoped that Daniel would be proposing to her. (She was correct.) On that Saturday, which was day #13 of their separation, Tess called Brother John, the man who ran the church's media station ministry. She explained the situation, and said that if Daniel should happen to propose to her in church on Sunday, would Brother John mind to flash one word, YES, on the big screen for everyone to see. Brother John said he was happy to oblige.

She did not know that two days earlier Daniel had called Brother John and placed his own request regarding the big screen. Brother John was as giddy as a kid in a candy store. His ministry as head of the media station team had never been so much fun.

Sunday morning when Tess walked into the sanctuary, Daniel was waiting for her in the center aisle, and not a soul in the room was whispering even a word. He had a jewelry box in his hand, the words on the big screen said:

```
God said YESS.
Marry me TESS.
-Daniel
```

As the whole church waited breathlessly for her to answer, Tess simply looked over at the media station, and with a knowing smile, she ever so slyly signaled Brother John to post her answer. Suddenly the church erupted in cheers. Daniel turned around in surprise to see the big screen saying:

```
YESS!
-TESS
```

Tess tingled with delight as Daniel opened the jewelry box and presented the ring to her. It was, of course, the very same ring that she had once accepted from him when they were small children.

Daniel said, "Please allow me to give you what was already yours."

In a nostalgic tease Tess said, "Do you want to marry me?"

"Yes," Daniel said.

"I've thought about it, and the answer is yes," said Tess. She held out her hand and permitted Daniel to place the ring onto her finger. She was practically glowing.

"OK," said Daniel, "So what did you bring for lunch today?"

"PB&J."

"Cool."

There are some moments in the Kingdom of God that are magical. This was one.

CHAPTER VI

Servants

Tess and Daniel were married in the fall. Tess's Uncle Percy gave her away in a straightforward ceremony in the church. Naturally the new couple lived in the house that Tess had inherited from the trust when her parents died.

Some might have said they were an odd couple. She was an ultra genius working toward a postgraduate degree at an age younger than anyone else ever had. He was a young preacher who had no reputation among the churches (he came from a family that had no preachers at all in it, let alone any well-known ones), a secular job that paid very little, and (from the point of view of any carnal person) no prospects for wealth, fame, or "success." Yet they loved God, and they loved each other.

Daniel pondered what he knew of the anti-religious atmosphere of the academic world at that time, and he decided that he and Tess ought to study for the purpose of preparing to defend Christianity against any attempts to thwart her faith through arguments of an academic or scientific nature. He trusted Tess completely, but he still felt they should study and prepare. One reason was that it occurred to him that Tess might find herself in a position to witness to academic people that others could not approach.

So Daniel read books by brilliant authors who showed scientific reasons to believe in a sovereign Creator. He read works by writers such as Meyer, Dembski, Johnson, Wells, and others, and then he discussed the issues with his wife and passed the books on to her. As Tess devoured the books, she began to remember little things that her father (who had been a scientist) had said to her. The issue quickly became important to her.

Before long Tess said, "I don't think my father believed in neo-darwinist evolution."

"Really?" Daniel asked, "What makes you say that?"

"Little things he would say. The tone of his voice. Sarcasm. Facial expressions. I am almost sure of it."

Soon afterward they happened to watch a documentary that showed how some scientists who had dared to write against neo-darwinism had been mistreated. Some had been denied tenure. Others had been fired, and, in some instances, blackballed in the scientific community. Tess contacted Don Tennyson, a scientist with whom her father had worked on several research projects. He had been a colleague and a trusted friend to her father.

Dr. Tennyson confided to Tess, "No, your father had done the math, and he knew the chemistry and the physics. He did not agree with any of the existing theories of accidental abiogenesis. He also considered the neo-darwinist premise [of unguided natural selection as the basis for all life forms] to be unsubstantiated. Your father sometimes feigned acceptance of it whenever he was around certain people in the academic community, but he never really bought into it. Just between you, me, and the fencepost, I don't buy it either. Please keep this between us. Heads have rolled and paychecks have been lost over this."

Tess witnessed to Dr. Tennyson about her experience with God and invited him to join them for Bible study.

Dr. Tennyson declined, then added, "I do believe that the universe and all life had an intelligent designer, but that does not translate into me thinking that any one religion knows who it is. The designer, or designers, may or may not be knowable by us. I guess you might call me an optimistic agnostic."

Tess said, "Setting aside a godless theory of abiogenesis is not enough. We each need to meet and embrace the Creator that many proponents of Intelligent Design refuse to identify. He's real. You can meet Him."

"No, thanks. I've never been one for religion, but thank you for asking. I'm flattered," he replied. His refusal was nothing new from those in the academic realm. Tess had gotten similar rejections more times than she could count.

She began to consider that if it were not for her tragic circumstances and Daniel's miraculous warning, her refusal of any offer of salvation might have been just as flat and unbending as the ones she was getting from those to whom she witnessed.

Daniel and Tess joined a group that sought to defend academic freedom regarding the issue of neo-darwinism, and they made a sort of personal hobby out of studying the topic. Daniel had no way of knowing that over a thousand years from that time, as an immortal, he would use some of the knowledge gained during their time of preparation in a speech he would deliver at a debate near the end of the Millennial Kingdom age.

Tess obtained her Master of Science degree. As Daniel drove her to Tenner Hall for the commencement ceremonies, he took them somewhat out of the way so as to avoid the bridge where the accident had occurred.

Tess affectionately patted him on the arm and said, "Thank you for bypassing the Callow bridge." She paused pensively, and then she said, "Ever since I was filled with the Holy Ghost, I have noticed that the allure of the academic system and the desire for more degrees is fading for me. I've decided to postpone any work toward a doctorate, perhaps indefinitely."

"That's fine, honey," Daniel said. "God is able to qualify His own for whatever service He requires. Beside that, even by human standards, you're already qualified for pretty much anything you might want to do."

The couple was soon drafted for teaching a Sunday School class, and they loved all the students as if they were their own. The Talbots were a huge asset to the Sunday School department, and over a period of many years they eventually taught practically every age group. Tess "mothered" each and every student, especially the little children. Both of them mentored the older children.

The pastor bestowed both responsibility and authority upon Daniel, who did everything from tedious grunt work behind the scenes, to preaching in the "limelight" where everyone could see.

"The call to the ministry of the Word brings with it a mixed bag, and you can't just pick and choose which parts you accept," Pastor Blaylock told him.

When the couple was called upon to serve in the office of youth pastor, they were some of the most dedicated servants to ever fill the post. Even after they had helped to develop younger couples to the point that they were able to hand the job over to someone else, they were still consulted often, and their leadership influence outlived, by a lifetime, their period of having the title.

The Blaylocks were tremendous. They taught and modeled servant leadership. They were true Christians from the inside out.

There came a day when Daniel was asked to become a full-time employee of the church. He accepted. Then came a day when Tess was asked to become a full-time employee of the church's school. She accepted. They served the church and school from then on. Daniel wore many hats and did whatever needed done. Tess soon became the principal of the Christian school. She found that working with the young students every day was, in a way, like being a mother. Sometimes she wondered if that might have been what the mysterious lady in white had meant by her prophecy.

Months began to slip by very quickly, and then years began to slip by even more quickly. Daniel seldom thought about the prophecy of the lady in white. When he did occasionally, he wondered how it might ever be fulfilled. Sometimes he pondered the fact that they only had a promise of Tess becoming a mother, not one of him also becoming a father. Yet if it was to be literally fulfilled, seemingly that would also need to happen. Oh, to ponder with hope. But how? When? In the meantime, there were many kids that they called their own, even if not biologically.

◆◆◆◆◆◆◆

There was a precious couple in their church, the Miltons, that did not buy into the modern, "small family" mentality that was so prevalent in the popular culture of the time. To top that, they did not give in to the cultural norm and economic pressures that duped so many women of that time into being focused on their careers instead of living family-oriented lives.

Daniel and Tess admired this particular couple because they simply refused to permit daycares and public employees to raise their kids just for the sake of being a two-career home and having that second income. The couple had a strong conviction that while men and women are equal in God's eyes, the biblical roles for the genders are different. The wife was a full-time homemaker. She home schooled all their children. The husband worked hard to provide for his family, and whenever money was sparse they simply tightened their belts and trusted God. He always saw them through.

Gradually Tess became aware that whenever news would spread that the couple was having "yet another one" (that is, the wife was pregnant with another child) the laughter of some of the mothers in the church was growing less and less joyous. In fact, it began to be tinged with mockery. This bothered her immensely. At first she could not put her finger on exactly what was wrong with their viewpoint, but the more she thought about it, the more sure she was.

It so happened that there was a fellowship dinner one Sunday, and afterward a crew of volunteers worked to clean up. Naturally Tess was among them. Near the end of the clean-up job, when almost everyone else had already left the building, a couple of mothers tried to engage Tess in a session of demeaning the couple that was having "too many" children. Their arrows were especially targeted toward the wife.

"I guess you knew that Tammy Milton is pregnant *again*," said the first one, Kim Keener. Twang. Swoosh. Thud. Direct hit.

"What is wrong with her brain?" said the second one, Michelle Brott. Twang. Swoosh. Thud. Another hit. It's amazing how verbal arrows can strike a victim who isn't even present to hear the words.

"I know!" Kim said. "It's like she thinks that women are supposed to just stay home, barefooted, and squeeze out kids. And it kills me when they gripe that money is tight for them. That's what Tammy says every time they go home when the rest of us go out. Instead of having so many kids, she needs to get a job. If she would get out and get a job like everybody else, then they could afford to do some fun stuff every now and then. Am I right, Tess?"

Tess could not believe what she was hearing. The two women did not even bother to look at her, or they would have seen her shaking her head with squinted eyes. As Tess was about to reply, the second woman, Michelle, launched another senseless strike in what promised to be an ongoing barrage of disparaging words.

Michelle said, "I guess the poor girl doesn't even realize that they invented birth control."

The two were so caught up in their smug conversation that they didn't even notice Tess until she turned to face them. They were so unaware of any wrongdoing on their part that they could not have anticipated Tess's response even if someone had tried to warn them. Kim smiled at Tess as though she expected Tess to join in their attack on Tammy Milton. Kim even reached toward Tess in a friendly way that said, *Hey, come on over here and join us!*

As Michelle finally noticed Tess she said, "Tess, maybe you can talk some sense into her. They're just going to be miserable until they stop and change their money situation."

Tess determined to not stand by for even one more of their snide remarks. She knew that they were totally wrong in more ways than she could count. Their mockery of others was unchristian, and their manner of turning another couple's birthrate count into a gossip-worthy event meant that their comments were classifiable as gossip. Moreover, there was something very anti-biblical about the anti-children worldview that they had accepted without question. Even that was not all. There was something else that Tess could not put her finger on. Tess lit into both of them with a well-deserved rebuke.

"What have the Miltons ever done to hurt either of you?" Tess said. "How does the size of their family hurt you? The Bible says that children are a blessing from God. The world thinks that children are a curse. I've listened to you talk. It sounds like you would agree with the world instead of the Bible. God Himself told human beings to be fruitful and multiply, and He's never taken that command back.

"So what if Tammy has decided to go for God's blessings—more children instead of less—and not go for the world's dangled carrot—a career outside the home and more money. So what? How does that hurt you? Why is that your business?

"Just because Tammy holds a conviction that you don't share does not give you the right to stand here and belittle her behind her back in sarcasm. You don't actually think that their family size is due to barefooted ignorance or lack of birth control. That was mean. You should be ashamed of yourselves.

"And another thing: Did you know that they're debt free? Making sure they stay that way gives them a very valid reason for eating at home so often. What has your eating out done for your family finances? Are you debt free? Is being in debt much fun?

"I don't buy the line that mothers who work outside the home are supposedly happier, smarter, wiser, and richer. Think about all the things that happen in their kids' lives that they miss and can never get back. Think about when they get old and alone and find out that no one from their career really cared or wants to be there for them then. That's when they change their mind about it, but it's too late. That's when they long for grandchildren that can never be born.

"It seems to me that kids from a two-parent family with a stay-at-home mom have a better chance of having a stable marriage and a good life. I think that kids without that usually face more of an uphill battle. Godly wisdom means finding out God's opinion on something and then living that way. God's opinion is clear. Children: Good. Debt: Bad. The world's opinion is the exact opposite. Think about it. Pray about it."

Michelle completely wilted under Tess's rebuke, but Kim quietly hid her defiance.

Finally Kim said firmly, "I'm sorry, but we obviously pushed a button or caught you at a bad time. We didn't mean to offend you. We'll see you later." She started motioning for Michelle.

Tess said, "OK, just let me say this. You didn't catch me at a bad time, but you did push a button. Now, I'm willing to listen to anything you have to say about what your convictions are and whether the Bible backs them up, but there is no call to make things personal by putting Tammy down like that."

Michelle walked away overwhelmed with guilt. Kim

went away angry and drove home talking to herself out loud.

"Who does she think she is?" Kim seethed, "Who is she to lecture me about motherhood? She has no kids. She works outside her house. And I can't believe she thinks my finances are any of her business! Who does she think she is? How dare she!"

Over time Kim's anger turned to hatred. Much later, Tess finally discovered that she had made a terrible enemy that day by standing up for truth and defending an innocent victim.

The church entered a frustrating cycle of making progress (seeing growth in numbers and maturity in members) only to lose ground in one dramatic crisis after another, in which seemingly stable families would just up and leave. Some transferred while others even turned away from God. Those in the church who were spiritual sensed that something was wrong. It was as though someone was going around starting little fires of discord and dissension. The church struggled to maintain unity and momentum.

After this had gone on for several months, Pastor Blaylock became desperate.

He told Daniel, "It's like we no sooner get one conflict resolved and get the emotional wounds dressed when we turn around and find another conflict, each one worse than before. We need to seek God and find out what's wrong."

The pastor publicly asked the church members to pray about these matters, and they scheduled a time of collective fasting. The people sought God. However, it was as though the heavens were made of brass. They could not get the Lord to make it stop.

Pastor and Sister Blaylock sat down with the Talbots, and the aging pastor said, "I've seen this once before. When I was young, there was a period when a church suffered terribly, because the Lord was sifting the people. The Lord used the devils as pawns, and in turn the devils used some of the people as pawns. The Lord sifted the people and removed many of them from the assembly. Afterward there came a great unity and a mighty revival. Those that could not be shaken loose saw real victory. Their church became very powerful. It's been strong ever since.

"I think that is what God is doing here. This undercurrent of problems and attacks will continue until the Lord has accomplished His purpose. We will simply have to trust in Him and ride out the storm."

Our dear reader may be aware that by God's wise choice, women's brains function very differently than men's. Women are capable of things that men cannot understand. For instance, women can often remember details that men cannot even notice, let alone commit to memory. So it was that Tess one day noticed something, a trend. Her observation turned out to be absolutely on target, but it boggled Daniel's mind that she had been able to piece it together.

Here is what she noticed: As one family after another either stopped attending the church or switched to some other church, Tess suddenly figured out that every married woman in whom she had ever noticed even a slight tinge of bitter mockery of Tammy Milton for her supposedly having too many children (back when Tess had rebuked Michelle and Kim so many months earlier), was now a woman whose family was being sifted right out of the church. Daniel and Tess pondered if any of those women's mockery of Tammy could possibly be a sin so grievous as to make God punish all those families. They both agreed that it was not grievous enough. There had to be something more. This was something bigger.

They pondered whether the backsliding ones had been truly saved; perhaps they had actually been faking faith even while yet attending church. If so, it seemed that would explain everything. What if these people were wolves in sheep's clothing? What if they either never were actually redeemed in the first place (they never fully surrendered to God), or were just secretly backslidden, or even worse—reprobate?

Tess told Daniel, "Remember what you said to me right after you were born again, about people being slaves who don't even know that they're slaves? I think that some of these people who are leaving us may be in that category. It may be that God is allowing this sifting to happen so perhaps some of them will finally be forced to confess to themselves the truth—that they're not saved—so they will finally be able to be saved. What appears to us like an attack that is damaging the church may actually be strengthening the church for the long term."

"I'll buy that," Daniel said, "but I'd love to know when this is going to end. Here's something else I'd love to know. Do all these people have something in common? Is there a single source who is being used to sour them, or is this just a bunch of unrelated, disconnected people?"

The Spirit of the Lord prompted Tess, and she said, "They do all have something in common. They were all friends with Brother and Sister Keener. There is a single source. It is Sister Kim Keener."

Tess dialed Sister Michelle Brott. She put her on the speaker phone so Daniel could hear.

"Hi, Sister Michelle. This is Sister Tess, and my husband is here with me. We need to ask you something very important. We need for you to answer honestly. I'm asking you this in Jesus name. *Has Sister Keener been saying things that have turned people against the pastor, or turned them away from the church?*"

Michelle paused for a long time, and then they heard her burst into sobs. For several seconds she said nothing.

When she finally regained a little bit of composure, in between sobs she said, "Yes. She hates you something awful, and she has secretly convinced a lot of people that you and Daniel are mean, lazy, dishonest, and—mean. She has been secretly telling a lot of people that there must be something wrong with Pastor Blaylock if he can't see through your lies. I know this because I have heard her say it. She tried to get me to believe it. For a while I did a little, but I don't now. I'm scared. Sister Tess, I'm scared. I think Kim may be demon possessed. I'm scared of her."

Daniel said, "I think we need to go meet with Pastor and Sister Blaylock about this."

They thanked Michelle for being honest and then ended the call. As they drove toward the Blaylock's home, the Lord suddenly spoke to Daniel. He pulled the car off the road, and then he called the pastor from his cell phone.

"Hello, Pastor," he said, "I have some good news and some bad news. The good news is that the Lord is almost done with the sifting. There is only one more family about to be affected. The—"

The pastor gently interrupted him, "The Keeners. I know. The Lord has just spoken to me, Brother Daniel."

"Yes, sir. One more thing. I'm just wanting to ask this for confirmation. I feel like the Lord just told me that—"

"That Kim Keener is committing adultery?"

"Yes sir."

"Yes, I'm sorry to say the Lord has just shown that to me also, Brother Daniel."

"Pastor, the Lord prompted me to take Tess and go to that big mall way over in Centenary, to—"

"—Get evidence, and to confront her," the pastor said, finishing Daniel's sentence for the third time. Then the pastor added, "Brother Daniel, be careful to remember the part about turning the other cheek."

"Sir? I don't understand."

"Well, if the Lord didn't tell you this part, He must have wanted me to tell you. The man that she's been seeing will be there. The Lord said for you to remember to turn the other cheek."

"Yes sir. I understand now. I'm getting back on the road. We'll call you soon. Bye."

After the call was ended Tess said, "That doesn't sound good at all."

Centenary was two hours away on a good day. However, since it was a Saturday, and there were so few shopping days left until Christmas, the traffic was horrible. It took them two and a half hours to get there. When they finally arrived at the shopping mall, they had to circle up to the second floor of the parking garage before they found an open spot. So they walked in on the second floor. Daniel told Tess to get her cell phone into video camera mode and be ready. After they were inside, they just started walking.

When they arrived at the handrail overlooking the food court below them (it was down on the first floor, yet all open above; the second floor did not cover it), they looked, and there beneath them, right beside the stairs, was Kim Keener, sitting at a table with a man who was definitely *not* her husband. Kim was dressed very immodestly, and she looked so worldly that they barely recognized her. She and the man were acting like infatuated, air-headed teenagers. They were unaware of anyone or anything around them. They were holding hands, laughing, and even kissing each other every so often.

Daniel pointed toward Tess's phone, but she was already recording. It only took seconds to get enough video footage to prove to anyone what was going on. Daniel motioned for her to keep recording as they got closer by going down the stairs. He held Tess's elbow as she both videoed and walked down the stairs at the same time. Halfway down the stairs, Daniel signaled for her to stop on a landing and keep on recording from there. He continued down the stairs and onto the main floor. Tess was close enough for her phone to pick up every word they were saying.

After a few more seconds, Daniel walked into the video frame. He very calmly said, "Hello, Kim. So, this is the man you've been sinning with. The—"

Suddenly the man at the table stood up, looked at Kim, and said, "Is this the guy? This is him, isn't it?"

The man then moved so fast that neither Daniel nor Tess could react fast enough. He suddenly hit Daniel with his fist, striking him hard on the left side of his jaw. Daniel had instinctively tried to sway to the right to avoid the blow, and so when the hit came he was already off balance. He went down. Kim put her hand over her mouth to muffle her own scream, and then she started yelling, "Bill, stop! That's not him! That's not my husband!"

As Tess came running down the stairs, Daniel got up off the floor and said, "Sir, I'm not who you thought I was, but the Lord has told me that I am supposed to turn the other cheek." Daniel leaned forward and offered the right side of his jaw.

The man instantly calmed down. He said, "Man, I'm so sorry! I thought— Any guy that would hit on a woman deserves to get beat up. I thought you were her husband!"

Tess (while still videoing) said, "Kim? You told him that Brother Buddy beats you? In the years we've known you, we have never seen a bruise or any marks. I'm having a hard time believing that accusation."

Kim grabbed her purse and ran away, across the food court and out through a side door. The man, Bill, was still apologizing.

Daniel said, "Sir, I am a preacher of the gospel, and we

came here today because the Lord told us that a member of our church was not what she seemed. He sent us here. My name is Daniel, and this is my wife, Tess. Would you mind to tell us how long Kim has been seeing you?"

The man bowed his head and said, "About six or seven months. Once or twice a week. Sometimes more."

"Well, she is married and a mother to two children, and her husband is a very nice guy who has probably not ever laid a hand on her in abuse or force. You may have been played."

By that time the man remembered that it had all been videoed, and he grew afraid of a lawsuit. He kept apologizing over and over, until Daniel and Tess finally convinced him that there were no hard feelings and that they were not going to sue him.

"Well, I'd better be getting back to the office," Bill said. "Again, I am sorry."

After he left, Daniel rubbed his jaw, which somehow was not quite as sore as he thought it would be, and he said, "I'm hungry. Here is food. What doth hinder us?"

"Oh, I don't know," Tess said, "got any broken teeth?"

Daniel dialed the pastor while they stood in line to get something to eat.

When Pastor Blaylock called Brother Buddy Keener and explained to him what had happened, Buddy was devastated. The next day, during the Sunday morning service, he was in attendance with the two children (a boy and a girl), but Kim was not there. Buddy looked exhausted. He had dark circles under his eyes. Daniel greeted him with a hug, as usual.

"We're praying for you, Brother Buddy," he told him.

Buddy whispered, "Kim never came home last night. She won't answer my voicemails. We have no idea where she is. I couldn't sleep. I can't believe this is happening. Not only that; I can't believe I never saw it coming. I should have. Last night I was going over stuff in my mind, and I think there were some signs that something wasn't right."

The earliest communication that Buddy had from Kim was four days later when she had him served with divorce papers. Later on she finally called, saying she wanted to talk to the kids, but she still did not return to the house physically. It was revealed that she had obtained a fully furnished apartment in Centenary. (She had done this long before her adulterous affair with Bill had been uncovered.) Buddy wondered how she could have withdrawn from her own house so suddenly unless there had been advance planning. He later learned that apparently there had been quite a bit of planning of some sort.

Kim had kept many secrets from her husband. Bill, the man with whom she had been fornicating, was an executive in the company where she worked. Kim had long flirted with Bill, and when she started telling him that she planned to divorce her violent husband and move on, Bill started trying to woo her in earnest. Eight months prior, Bill had been largely responsible for her receiving a big promotion and a huge raise. She had not ever told her husband about the extra money, which she kept hidden in a secret account that she had opened at a bank over in Centenary. Soon afterward she had leased the apartment. There she and Bill had gone to commit their adulterous acts. She steadily amassed a secret collection of very worldly clothes that no one in her family or the church ever saw. She had two dwellings, two wardrobes, and two men. Yet she loved one and hated the other.

Although she had attempted to lead a double life, she became cold and aloof toward her husband, and she ceased all relations with him in their marriage bed. She also had openly shown signs that she despised him. At times she had tried to provoke him, almost as if she wanted to drive him to become violent so that her own lie would become true. Yet Buddy had never hit her.

The pastor and the church board met to discuss the matter of Kim's membership status in the church and whether Brother Buddy had biblical grounds for divorce and could therefore remarry without it being a sinful act. Buddy and Kim were asked to be present to address the board, and Daniel and Tess were asked to come and testify. All of them came to the meeting except for Kim.

Daniel and Tess testified, and they presented the video evidence. Buddy was given a chance to speak, and then the board discussed the matter. Finally they officially declared that Kim's membership in the church was null and void, and that Buddy had justifiable grounds for divorce and therefore the right to remarry. They also provided Brother Buddy with a letter for the secular courts in which they recommended that custody of the children be awarded to him.

While Kim refused to show up for a hearing at the church regarding salvation, she was present for the secular divorce hearings regarding money and child custody. In a judgment that astounded many, the divorce court judge awarded custody of the two Keener children to Kim. Buddy was only to get them every other weekend. Buddy appealed the decision, but he was not able to prevail. Daniel identified with the feelings of helplessness that Buddy suffered. It reminded him of his time of feeling helpless after Tess's accident years earlier. Although Daniel and Tess lived every single day with the nagging pain of being childless, Tess said that even she was not sure she could imagine the pain of having one's children wrongfully taken away.

There is an old saying that bad news can travel around the world while good news is still trying to lace up its shoe. The news of Kim's sin and shameful departure spread quickly, both to the families remaining in the church and to many of those who had left the church. However, not only the salacious parts were told, but also the ominous details of the hand of God at work in the matter. Kim was not there to spin the matter her way, except in the instances where she stayed in contact with some of the backsliders that were favorable to her side in the issue.

During the months that followed, some of the families that had departed eventually saw that they had been mis-led about Pastor and Sister Blaylock and about Daniel and Tess, and they knew they were wrong in leaving. Some of the families ultimately returned. Of those that never came back, several more divorces resulted. The sift-ing trial forever changed the assembly, but in the end, it was for the best. The church became very strong in unity and experienced great growth.

The Blaylocks did much to help Daniel and Tess. The two couples loved one another dearly. In the absence of her own parents, Pastor and Sister Blaylock became somewhat of a father figure and mother figure for Tess. Daniel's own father was a very ungodly man, so Pastor Blaylock was the godly, spiritual, father figure that Daniel had sorely needed.

Two decades went by in a flash. The Blaylocks grew very old. Several years prior to Brother Blaylock's death, he guided the church to elect Daniel as their pastor, and

Bishop Blaylock became senior pastor. Daniel found that serving the church as pastor was not a threat of stress because Bishop Blaylock was still alive. The elder minister's presence was a safety net that drained all fear and worry out of a task that would have been very daunting otherwise.

It finally came to pass on a brisk November morning that God called Brother Blaylock home to glory. The whole church mourned the passing of a hero. Many people from the community came to pay tribute. As they laid Pastor William Blaylock's elderly remains to rest in the ground, Daniel and Tess wept uncontrollably.

Daniel was then the spiritual authority in that strong local church. The Talbots worked to mentor and develop other couples just as the Blaylocks had mentored them.

Before her own death two years later, Sister Blaylock instituted a saying that was taken up by all the church people. They said that, "Sister Tess is the best mother in the church." The saying always made Tess laugh. She had never dreamed she would ever become a pastor's wife. There were still those occasions when she felt pangs of regret over the lack of biological children of their own, but their life of service in the Kingdom of God was so profoundly fulfilling that she thanked God daily for giving Daniel to her and thanked Him for saving them both.

◆◆◆◆◆◆

There was a man in the church who was formerly military. His actual name was Havill Camoy, but everyone just called him "Steed." Among all of God's people anywhere, he was one of the most interesting. He became a dear friend to Daniel and Tess, and they accompanied him on several wonderful trips to Israel. Of all the things they experienced during their mortal lives, very few were as fulfilling as their trips to the holy land.

During their first trip they found a little café near the Jafa Gate that became their favorite place to eat while staying in Jerusalem. On the day they discovered the little café, they had backpacked all over the steep hilly area around the city. (Jerusalem is a city set on a mountain, and it is surrounded by mountains.) As they hiked back toward their rooms they were exhausted and starved. When they saw the café and decided to check it out, they had no idea they were about to taste the most delicious food they had ever eaten. Likewise, the owner and the chef (and other employees) had no idea that they were about to meet the most grateful customers they had ever seen.

Based on a glowing recommendation, they all ordered the same menu item, called Shishlik. It was a dish they had never heard of, which consisted of skewers of spice-coated chicken breast and lamb's meat roasted over an open flame, served with handmade hummus and a fresh Arabic salad consisting of diced tomato, diced cucumber, chopped mint leaf, and other spices. Delicious pita bread was provided so that all the ingredients could be combined into sandwiches the likes of which they had never tasted. Daniel had also requested something spicy, and so they were brought a large bowl of homemade, semi-liquid pepper sauce for all to share. A few seconds into the meal, the tiny group of tourists was so overwhelmed with how good the food was that they began to exclaim they had never tasted anything so wonderful.

Steed, a very outgoing guy, suddenly announced, "This meal is worthy of a standing ovation. Who's with me?"

At that, he stood up and began to clap and cheer. Everyone at the table clapped their hands and shouted. Several of them stood up, and a couple whistled loudly.

The owner smiled broadly and bowed his head in gratitude. The chef came from the kitchen in back to see what the commotion was, and at his appearing the owner held up his hands toward the chef, gesturing that he was the one worthy of the applause. So everyone redoubled their cheering, and the group became louder than ever. It was the first time the tiny restaurant had ever experienced such an ecstatic reception, and the chef turned beet red as he smiled and bowed low several times in acknowledging the accolades. From then on they visited the café every day while they stayed in Jerusalem.

Steed was so enthusiastic with regard to witnessing that Daniel and Tess seemed mild by comparison. He began to witness to the café owner and his staff. Daniel and some of the other brothers were quick to join in.

One day they approached the café to eat there, only to find it closed. The next day when they came back they asked the owner why the restaurant had been closed the day before. He explained that he had been at the hospital for several tests. He was a sick man. They gathered around him and prayed for him to be healed. He was grateful for the prayers. Indeed the Lord did heal him.

By the time Daniel, Tess, Steed and the others finally departed from Jerusalem, they had introduced the café owner to a local Christian church there in the city. This eventually resulted in three people coming to the Lord.

The habit of cheering for the delicious food became a bit of a tradition among the little party of tourists. Those believers never imagined that hundreds of years into the future, during the Millennial Kingdom age, they would continue that same tradition, only with a completely different owner and staff, while the same café was operating under a different name.

Bishop and Sister Blaylock had taught many wonderful lessons to Daniel and Tess, but it was Steed who taught them to be more reckless in faith. Over their years of friendship, Steed often did things for God that seemed crazy, yet time and again God honored Steed's faith and did amazing things through him. It was a great lesson for them to learn.

◆◆◆◆◆◆◆

Daniel and Tess just happened to be together when they heard the sound of the trumpet that marked the catching away of the Bride of Christ. There was a split second that seemed to pass in slow motion as they clasped hands just before their change occurred.

Detail of plan for rebuilt temple in Jerusalem, Israel.

CHAPTER VII

Thy Kingdom Come

Coming into the Millennial Kingdom age was a traumatic transition for mankind on the Earth. The unbridled wickedness of men and the presence of demonic forces in the world resulted in such an outpouring of God's wrath that the horrible mess prior to the Rapture seemed like a cake walk when compared to the great Tribulation. Yet for believers such as Daniel and Tess, there was no stress at all in the transition. They were changed into immortal beings and translated to the heavenly Jerusalem, and thus they were not present on the Earth during all of the outpouring of God's wrath.

What a glorious reunion they had with the Blaylocks as well as many others they had known previously. There was an austere ceremony in which the Lord Jesus personally assigned a new and secret name to every redeemed immortal, and He bestowed upon them all a gift—a white stone with their new name written inside it. Tess's academic commencements seemed like child's play in contrast to this awesome ceremony of "graduation." However, their educations were far from complete.

At the end of the great Tribulation they, along with a mighty host of other saints from across the ages, accompanied the Lord Jesus back to the Earth. There they helped the Lord to reshape and rebuild life for the nations of people who were permitted to survive the Tribulation and enter into the Millennial Kingdom.

One of the most stark differences was the absence of any demonic presence upon the Earth. Those mortal people born after the removal and imprisonment of the spirits of fallen angels (commonly called devils or demons) had no frame of reference with which to compare the idyllic state of the world during their time. They could not really understand what it used to be like. Instead of human spirits continually being mauled, tricked, intimidated, and manipulated by demonic spirits, the people of the world enjoyed peace. The whole Creation seemed to heave a sigh of relief.

The Lord Jesus spent part of His time tutoring the mortal citizens of the world and coaching His immortal followers in their additional tutoring of the nations. (He appointed redeemed immortals to rule over the nations as part of His campaign to rid the world of wars and conflicts.) Yet He also spent part of His time teaching powerful skills to the redeemed immortals. In many cases, He taught key immortals who were then entrusted with teaching other immortals. He taught them secrets about space-time that were previously unimagined, while He shored up their understanding in other areas in which they needed more maturity or more wisdom.

Daniel and Tess began to learn such things as how to teleport, and how to "go between" (some new immortals called it 'tweening) which refers to manipulating the phase of things (in relation to the normal phase of space-time). 'Tweening permits such activities as flying, hovering, and becoming invisible.

With the devils bound, the false religions disproved, and the evil powers and wicked authorities overthrown, the mortal people found themselves in a whole new world, in a fairly literal sense. There was much work to be done, and every redeemed immortal had multiple duties. Their tasks were important, and their responsibilities were weighty. Yet, because of their trust in God and their well-suited levels of skill, they endured little stress, and what concerns they did have were not able to inflict physical damage to them, as had been the case back when they were still mortal.

Daniel and Tess were part of a small minority among all the redeemed immortals: They were among the few who had never physically died. The general rule for all of the fallen descendents of Adam and Eve is "it is appointed unto men once to die, but after this the judgment." Those few who had been caught away before death included Enoch and Elijah from the Old Testament as well as all the raptured New Testament saints. They were the exception to the rule, which was a point that did not often matter in the hereafter, yet it could occasionally become rather important.

Although Daniel and Tess knew (from an intellectual standpoint) that their marriage to each other concluded when they became immortal (when they consummated their eternal marriage to the Lord), for the first two or three hundred years they still felt related to one another like a happily married couple who simply had separate mansions. Although their love for each other never diminished, over time their love for other souls, both immortal and mortal, increased in proportion to their love for one another. Also, their eternal state of being married to the Lord Jesus Christ (instead of to each other) caused their relationship with Him to take center stage in a way that eclipsed all other relationships.

God knew that Tess would gain tremendous fulfillment from working with mortal children (especially orphans and the terminally ill), and so that was a big part of her life. He also tasked her with teaching some heavy-duty concepts of physics (including some mind-boggling information that He taught her) to a key team of immortals who were not only going to eventually need to know that information, but who also were tasked in turn with teaching other immortals as well.

Daniel's calling as a preacher in the prior life carried over into preaching in the Millennial Kingdom age. On various occasions either the Lord or His people arranged appointments for Daniel to expound on various important concepts of citizenship and service in the Kingdom. Daniel's love of study was stronger than ever, and he enjoyed very direct access to the Lord as a source of information, as well as volumes of information that were beyond his reach as a mortal.

Both Daniel and Tess completely dismissed their earlier thoughts about becoming parents. Since immortals neither marry, nor are they given in marriage, they both justifiably assumed that becoming immortal before ever becoming parents meant that they were never going to become biological parents. They both felt that they were simply among the number of humans throughout history for which that simply was not meant to be. In fact, they were so sure that they never even asked the Lord about it. Had they asked, He might have told them something of His plan.

One of the study groups led by Tess specialized in advanced applications of some of what the Lord had revealed to them about space-time. The group consisted of immortals who were well suited to their tasks. Their entire history of intellect and knowledge (even during their time as mortals) had prepared them for study in areas that other immortals might never need and would seldom bother with.

They began to focus on the difference between teleporting to and fro on the Earth versus translating themselves between the Earth and the heavenly Jerusalem. The two kinds of jumps came easily for all immortals, but the study group began to consider that the heavenly Jerusalem seemed to be a distinct space-time; not part of the space-time of the universe as they knew it.

They postulated that in a very real way, every time an immortal translated himself from the heavenly Jerusalem to the Earth (or vice versa), that immortal was actually traveling between two discrete pockets of space-time.

As they pondered on this, the ramifications regarding the possibilities of time travel became a concern. None of these rather scholarly immortals needed to be lectured about the problems of causality loops or the dangers of corrupting the timeline of history on the Earth.

Tess was the most skillful among them with regard to controlling a jump portal's points of entry and exit, and it was decided that Tess would try to succeed in a jump that not only traversed "where" but also "when." She knew to be careful not to do anything that would change the timeline.

Tess made the jump, and she found herself standing in her own world, within her own childhood neighborhood at some point in the past. It was incredibly familiar to her, yet it was being seen from a certain vantage point from which it had technically not been seen by her while she was still mortal, so it was both familiar and unfamiliar all at once.

She was standing within sight of her old elementary school from childhood. As she looked across the schoolyard, she saw children playing. She walked over and leaned against the fence, studying details to pin down the "when" of that moment. Suddenly the realization came. It was the day a young boy, Daniel, had given a stolen engagement ring to a tiny girl, Tess, on the playground. She watched with awe as the younger version of herself received the ring.

As this fact dawned on her, she saw one of the teachers on duty, Mrs. Ronstadt, pointing toward her and saying something.

Uh oh, Tess thought. *Time to go.*

In the split instant when Mrs. Ronstadt turned her head toward the childhood Tess, the immortal Tess teleported back to her own time.

She told the others, "It worked. I actually went back to my own past, and watched myself as a small child. I was seen by an adult and almost seen by the earlier version of myself as well as by the boyhood version of Daniel, the man whom I later married and who, as you all know, is now immortal. It was— It was unnerving and probably tremendously dangerous. I'm charging all of us to not ever try this again unless the Lord has specifically told us to do so."

They all agreed, and none of them had to be compelled. They were not people who had to experience something to believe it was real, and they had no desire to change or undo anything in the past. They were simply ecstatic to learn that their understanding was correct and the knowledge they had gained might one day be useful.

One day while Tess was working with a group of orphans at a clinic, she explained to them about the white stone that they all could get one day, if they trusted in the Lord and served Him with all their hearts. She went to her desk and brought out her white stone and showed it to them. She asked them what they saw inside it. The answers ranged from "shimmering lights" to "dancing colors." She smiled and explained to them that only the person to whom the stone is given can see his or her own new name inside.

She told them, "There is no sense in anyone trying to find out my secret name by stealing my white stone, because all they would see is just shimmering lights or dancing colors."

However, what she did not take into account was that shimmering lights and dancing colors were quite enough to make some mortal children want to steal her white stone. One orphan girl in the group that day immediately coveted Tess's white stone. The girl, named Tarinda, carefully watched where Tess placed the stone when she returned it to her desk. Tess had taught that same lesson to many such groups without ever having a problem. The very reason she kept the stone there at her desk instead of back at her mansion in the heavenly Jerusalem was for convenience sake in teaching that lesson to mortal children.

Several days later, Tess was teaching phase manipulation of particle streams to a group of immortals when she became aware of a strange feeling.

"Is something wrong?" one of them asked.

"I think so," she said, "but I don't know exactly what."

She inwardly asked the Lord what was wrong, and He revealed to her that what she sensed was that Tarinda had stolen her white stone. He showed her that if she concentrated, she would be able to sense the location of the stone and teleport it back to herself. She did so.

The group of immortals that she was teaching saw her reach into a portal and pull her white stone out. On the other end of the portal, Tarinda saw a hand come out of nowhere and take the stone back.

"Everything is just fine now," she said, "except I still need to deal with a little thief later. I won't be too hard on her."

Tess got back into her lesson, in which she was showing the group how light could be taken out of phase momentarily, therefore having it unblocked by a table, whose shadow on the floor correspondingly had a hole in it while she demonstrated. As she explained the principles at work, she thought about the hand-through-a-portal reach she had just used to retrieve her white stone, and she inwardly wondered if some angel had done something similar long ago when a hand came from nowhere and wrote strange words for King Belshazzar on the wall: "Mene, Mene, Tekel, Upharsin."

CHAPTER VIII

Surati

The Corlan marry and never divorce. When the Corlan reproduce, it is always on a set schedule. (In fact, all the other creatures on Sset reproduce on the same schedule as well.) Once per every twelfth cam (which translates to just over 116 of our years, if accounting for the time rate differential between the two universes), during some portion of the C'alimnet event and its accompanying festival, all the married couples lock themselves away in private and perform a very intimate, secretive reproductive ritual for each other. It is a very private matter.

As God would have it, the younger Corlan are not given any memories of their ancestors performing this ceremony and ritual until they mature to the point of c'ali (which is the Corlan word that essentially means puberty). Those particular memories simply are not written by the surati into a Corlan's long-term memory until needed. A hormone secreted by the host Corlan at just the right time signals the surati to create the memories.

C'ali occurs for maturing Corlan men and women during their twelfth cam—during their first C'alimnet festival. The Corlan may marry prior to their c'ali, and they are encouraged to do so. Any Corlan who is not already married by the time of his or her own c'ali always gets married between their c'ali and the very next C'alimnet festival.

When a married couple mates during C'alimnet, it *always* results in a conception. In the entire history of the Corlan, there has never been a failed mating attempt. There has never been a wasted ova, or a wasted sperm, or a miscarriage. They suffer no birth defects.

During the latter portion of the gestational period that follows, the Corlan couple both instinctively secrete a hormone that signals the surati microbes within them to copy the M-DNA while they replicate themselves as needed. The newly formed surati assemble in a way that will preserve and transmit a complete copy of all their prior ancestors' memories, together with the memories added in their current host's own lifetime up to that point. The assembled surati (containing all the memories) then travel (similar to how an infection would travel through our bodies) to their host's sinus cavity and oral cavity. In the mother, even her breast milk can eventually contain new surati, if the transfer should ever be delayed too long.

When the child is born, there is a ritual in which the mother and father both thoroughly chew (but do not swallow) a fruit called *mnet* (pronounced "uhm-*net*") that is available around the time of C'alimnet. The mnet fruit is tasteless at first, but when the new surati residing within their host's saliva then enter into the fruit, the mnet turns sweet and takes on a delicious flavor. This is caused by the surati breaking down the composition of the mnet as they draw nourishment from it that will enable them to spread out and find their place within the new child who is to be their host.

So the mother and father chew the mnet until it gets its flavor (by that point in time it is thin and runny), and then they feed the partially digested, surati-infused mnet fruit to their newborn. As the soft, delicious, semi-liquid fruit is enjoyed by the baby, the surati spread out and find their new home. Traditionally the same spoon, called *mnetsu*, is used by both parents to symbolically illustrate that the new child is to get both parents' memories, even though the child will only be using the memories from his or her parent of the same gender. The reason for transferring memories the child will never use is that he or she can eventually pass the other parent's memories to his or her own child that might be of the other gender.

The ceremony continues with other deeds that provide additional, redundant ways by which the surati may be physically transferred to the newborn. One is when the mother and father ceremonially kiss their newborn on the forehead and on both cheeks. Another is cuddling the newborn's bare skin against their own. The warm embrace is soothing to both parent and child, and yet serves a dual purpose that is both ceremonial and able to transfer the memory microbes. Still another, which is a little touch often added to the ceremony "just to make sure" is when the mother and father actually lick their fingers and anoint the baby's forehead with a little bit of their saliva.

Some of the ceremonial process is clearly more than is physically necessary for the transfer to occur. The general idea is "better safe than sorry." In most cases the transfer could still occur even if one parent messed up badly during the ceremony (which has never happened). Even that still might not be enough to stop the complete transfer, because as the father and mother have kissed previously (around the time of the birth), their new surati will have combined and the united memory microbes from the father and mother will have spread across the skin surface of both. Thus their combined surati can be transmitted to the new baby by even just a touch from only one of the loving parents.

It is easy to see that the surati were designed to make it exceedingly difficult for the parents to fail in transferring the memories. Consider that even if the parents were to administer mnet fruit that was not yet infused, *and* even if they did not kiss the baby, *and* even if they did not rub the baby's skin against theirs, *and* even if they did not each anoint the baby with some of their saliva, *and* even if all their touches were against the baby's clothes or blankets instead of his or her skin, *still* the surati could eventually (over the course of a few days or so) spread out over the surfaces of inanimate objects or plant matter and finally reach the baby. In such a case there would likely be some holes eaten into various household items as the surati gathered the needed resources to keep multiplying, but the transfer would likely still happen.

There have been rare instances of such an occurrence when the parents delayed the ceremony, and their new surati multiplied so quickly that they spread beyond the parents bodies and began to devour items in the home (blankets, clothing, plants, etc.) until they found their newborn host.

Surati spreading in this way will not enter into any Ssettian animals, nor will they enter into a Corlan who already has surati of his or her own inside. When they reach the newborn baby, they are able to tell whether the baby is free of any surati, meaning it is the right child.

They will pass over other Corlan until they find the one who is free of any surati of his or her own.

No one but God knows how the surati communicate across distances, but it seems they can. Once any of the new surati find the proper place (their new host child), all the other new surati of the same strain (whether still present on the parents or anywhere else) then become inert. Corlan scientists have studied this communication ability to no avail.

The substance is normally invisible, but in massive quantities it becomes visible as a slightly pink, mucus-like covering. If the parents have delayed the ritual far too long, this covering can sometimes be seen on the skin of the parents or perhaps eating away at their clothing or other household objects. In such cases it turns a faintly neon shade of purple once any of the new surati finally reach the baby. Then the purple, inert surati (which no longer need to search for the baby) quickly become a dry, flaky powder that can be brushed away.

In the extremely rare instances when a new parent is seen disposing of partially eaten clothing or any other such evidence, the offending couple is teased as being a *suratisot* (a foolish one [who waited too long] regarding the surati). Such teasing is usually lighthearted, but often it is tinged with an undercurrent of emotion, because the word of the Lord to the Corlan made it very clear that they are just one sin away from corruption and calamity.

◆◆◆◆◆◆

At this point we should make the reader aware of several important bits of information:

The first Corlan, Shao, was once carried here to our universe, and brought to our own planet by the Lord via an angelic visitation. The Lord brought the couple here to show them our world's sin-cursed state, in order to give them an understanding about how terrible the effects of sin are. The recollection of that visit is stark and clear for all Corlan that are old enough to have obtained that memory.

Although the Corlan are a noble people of profound innocence, they still possess freedom of choice, even freedom to sin. Just as Adam and Eve in our universe (in the Garden of Eden, prior to their sin) possessed the freedom to disobey, so also every Corlan possesses the same freedom. During their rich history, there have been occasional arguments, disagreements, and situations that needed to be addressed, but the Elders among them have always ruled well, and thus no major confrontations have ever developed and no discord or anger has ever lingered long.

Here in our world, God's teaching to us (in Ephesians 4:26) says two important things about anger: "In your anger do not sin" and "Do not let the sun go down while you are still angry." God had issued a similar kind of teaching to the Corlan. Yet consider how important that doctrine is for them, since during their sleep the surati are depending on an environment unclouded by the confusing brain chemistry that lingering anger causes.

God issued one crucial commandment to all the Corlan. He did this by commanding the first Corlan, Shao, before they had any children. That command, which pertained specifically to their kind in their universe, was this: "You shall not withhold the memories."

To stress the dire importance of the command, God explained that in the day that any Corlan ever withheld the memories, all Corlan would pay for the sin of that one. God told Shao, "You may divide the dwelling places. You may divide the language (although you ought not). However, you must not ever withhold the memories."

The next point is related to the fact that no creature on Sset had ever died. The entire family of Ssettian creatures all reproduced on a set schedule, and the timing and pace at which the surati microbes multiplied was specifically matched to the timing and pace at which new Corlan babies were born. Every Ssettian cell had a purpose and had a way in which to serve and fulfill that purpose. In the case of the surati cells, any lack of a proper host for which to serve and fulfill their purpose would be a disaster. The awesome power of the living substance would be turned into a terrific blight of destruction if the commandment of God was ever broken—if a curse of disobedience ever resulted in surati with no Corlan for which to fulfill their purpose.

Finally, God's words to Shao not only commanded them what not to do, but He also foretold that one day His commandment would be broken and that the people would perish. This would be due to the coming of the wicked Ettosedondi. Yet even in the prophecy of the Ettosedondi there was some hope given. God added that He would send a deliverer to preserve the Corlan memories, and that all those Corlan who died in innocence, without having sinned against God, would be raised to life again in a way that could not ever be undone. Every living Corlan both feared, and took comfort from, this part of the prophecies.

The Council Chambers of the Elders, at the heart of the Corlan society.

CHAPTER IX

Ettosedondi

uring their twenty-sixth C'alimnet, the eldest Corlan, Shao, turned 312 cam of age—which would translate to almost 3,021 of our years. In that cam's festival the Corlan population grew from just under 41,000 to over 61,000. It was the first C'alimnet in their entire history that their world, Sset, was unable to see all of the stellar event, because the latter portion of it was eclipsed by T'and (the gas giant) coming between them and the event. It was an omen of grave significance.

One of the babies that was conceived during the festival was a male named S'traf. His parents dutifully transferred the memories to him. As he matured, it was seen that he was exceptionally bright. There had never been such an intelligent Corlan. Everyone hailed him for his ability to add more technical knowledge and scientific understanding to his collective memory stream than any other Corlan had before. Also, he possessed cleverness that made better use of the memories than ever before in someone so young. As occasional situations arose that required the judgment of the Elders, a few of the Corlan began asking S'traf his opinion on the matter. Eventually some Corlan came straight to him to have him judge a matter instead of taking it before the Elders. S'traf was very sincere, but he began to be proud.

S'traf and his betrothed, *J'rel*, were married prior to their c'ali. She was perhaps the most beautiful bride ever in Corlan history, and she came from a respected family with a distinguished history. In accordance with Corlan tradition, the one name of the new couple was Straf. (The male's name loses its *dri*, which is represented here as an apostrophe, and the female adopts and shares the new name. The husband and wife are distinguished in spoken language by tone of voice and in written language by a difference in writing style, similar to our font differences between normal typeface and *italics* typeface.)

Straf began to nurse an idea that he conjured: Since the memory stream was growing longer and longer, the Corlan were getting better and better. In particular, the younger Corlan who had access to the longer memory stream at an earlier age were (in his view) the most capable and wisest Corlan. Since the younger Corlan were obviously getting better and wiser than the Elders, he thought the younger Corlan should rule instead of the Elders. In his pride, he sincerely believed the Corlan species would be better off when ruled by him, rather than by the Elders.

He approached the eldest, Shao, along with the other Elders. He explained his idea. They wisely and tactfully rejected it, while carefully informing him of why. They explained that a young Corlan's ancestral memory stream is disjointed. It contains only a portion of each ancestor. They pointed out that the eldest, Shao, possessed a continuous memory stream of actual experiences spanning a longer time than that of any other Corlan. He was not only the father of all Corlan, but he was also a prophet to whom God spoke. He was God's appointed judge and ruler.

Straf refused to hear their points. His pride blinded him to reason. They tried to dissuade him from his wrong beliefs, but he became defiant. From his pride sprang anger, which was also quickly accompanied by bitterness. In this negative state of mind, his wrong beliefs soon led to a plan for wrongful action. The stage was being set for the terrible sin that God had foretold long ago.

Straf left the council chambers of the Elders intent on proving that he was right, since the Elders obviously lacked the wisdom to see it for themselves. He waged a campaign intent on gaining supporters. It was described in polite political terms, yet it was actually rebellious. However, while he was blinded to his own bitterness, pride, anger, and hatred, the other Corlan were not blind. None of them would follow him. He finally settled into a stonewalled stance of silence. His wife was his only supporter. Even she inwardly doubted him, and she increasingly suppressed a terrible sense of dread about him.

In his bitterness, Straf's thinking literally became warped. Prolonged anger and hatred caused his endocrine system to produce and release chemicals into his body and brain that no Corlan had ever experienced for any considerable length of time. His surati became confused by these chemical imbalances, and therefore Straf stopped getting new memories each night. For the first time in his life, and the first time in Corlan history, the flow of memories was completely halted. Memories that had already been transferred in M-DNA format ceased being translated into long-term memories. In his anger, Straf was withholding the memories from himself.

Instead of becoming alarmed about a serious problem within himself and then seeking healing, Straf simply took note of how many of his recent fathers' memories were not yet bestowed within him, and he began to wonder if those fathers had indeed somehow broken the commandment and had withheld the memories. At first he felt betrayed, which led to further emotional disturbance.

With increased self-exposure to harmful emotions

that produced detrimental results, his surati became warped and bewildered. The microbes began to attack his long-term memory during his sleep, eating away and destroying his memories instead of adding new ones. Instead of receiving coherent signals, the protein nanites in his surati were getting nothing but static and confused babbling from their host microbes, and they began to assemble sections of randomness within the M-DNA that contained his own personal memory stream. With each additional day of his prolonged hatred, Straf was destroying a precious commodity: his own mind. He became more and more delusional. In his perverted state, he had finally become the Ettosedondi. He was the enemy of the Corlan. He was set to become the downfall and destruction of his kind.

In his downward spiral of delusion, Straf convinced himself that some of his fathers had withheld the memories from him, and that must be the reason why his intellectual ability was greater than that of others, and why he was a better Corlan than all the rest. He used this explanation to justify his decision to withhold the memories. He determined to prove that God's command was foolishness and that his way was better. He became convinced that a Corlan child who was born and raised without the memories would be the brightest, smartest, wisest Corlan ever. He suspected that his wife distrusted and feared him, so he withheld his plan from her.

Lower right: Telmis Observatory, used to observe moons and the sedondi.

CHAPTER X

Destruction

The Corlan were all gathering for the twenty-seventh C'alimnet event and festival. It would mark Shao's 324th cam (which is over 3,137 of our years). Their scientists who studied the sky predicted that it would be the first C'alimnet event in their history that would be entirely eclipsed from view by T'and. They were to miss not only part, but all of the event as far as visual perception was concerned. Their astronomers were correct. Nevertheless, all the married couples were preparing to find a time during the fellowship and feasting when they could slip away and lock themselves in for the secret, intimate reproductive ritual. In that cam's festival, the Corlan population was to grow from less than 62,000 to over 92,000.

Corlan couples who married prior to their own c'ali (that is to say, before their first C'alimnet event, during which their own puberty occurred) had an advantage over those who did not. Instead of experiencing their c'ali (and gaining the memories of the mating ritual) without any spouse of their own, and then having to wait for twelve more cam to pass before being able to finally enjoy the experience, they could both undergo their c'ali and enjoy the mating ritual with their spouse during the same event.

When the c'ali happened for Straf, the wife got the memories, but the demented husband did not. Knowing that he needed his wife's continued trust in him, he managed to stop himself from incoherent mumbling. He put on a good show for her. He hoped to get crucial information from her since she had gotten the memories. However, he had approached the event thinking that he needed both the memories and the physical changes of the c'ali in order to procreate. He was the first Corlan to discover that the physical changes alone gave him instinctive urges within his body that made him capable of the physical act of procreating, although the lack of the memories made it impossible for him to properly appreciate anything or participate in a way that was intimate and caring. To put it bluntly, the physical occurrence of c'ali combined with the lack of the memories made him capable of raping his spouse.

Yet, out of a sordid curiosity, he sought to have his wife divulge to him the memories anyway; he wanted the details of the intimate ritual. He coyly hinted that he had gotten the memories as well, and that he already knew the ceremonial aspects of the wonderful time they had in mind, but he sought the joy of hearing his wife talk about it.

Straf obliged him. She mentioned this detail and that, while trying to believe (against her better judgment) that he was not as ill as he seemed, and that perhaps he was getting back to normal after all.

They performed the physical aspect of the ritual and bonded in a way that would produce a child. That aspect of the joining worked as intended, and *Straf* (the wife) conceived. However, Straf (the husband) did a poor job of faking his way through the ceremonial aspects of what should have been a cherished, intimate ceremony. The name S'tael was chosen for the baby by the mother.

As the gestational period of the pregnancy neared completion, Straf (the husband) tried to maintain his fake show of civility, but his wife noticed that he would not ever kiss her, and that he refused to even touch her. He was withholding the memories.

Straf was distraught. She prayed continually for a miracle, but she was asking amiss, for she was, in effect, praying for God to overthrow her husband's freedom of will, to take away his option of choosing to sin. Such a prayer cannot ever be answered in the way that the praying believer hopes it will, because God long ago decreed that all innocents created in His image possess the freedom to choose between obedience and rebellion.

The moment her baby was born, *Straf* reached to embrace him, but her husband was too fast. He covered the child in a blanket and carried him out, amidst his wife's sobs and begging of him to stop. The hopeless mother gathered herself as quickly as she could. She tried to follow her husband, but he had fled so quickly that by the time she was able to pursue there was no trace of them. She had no idea which way he had gone or where he was going. She began a frantic search. She was determined that she would not stop until she found them.

While his infant son screamed for his mother's milk and cried for sweet mnet fruit, Straf swiftly carried his firstborn away into the mountains, resolved to raise his ultra genius son without the "curse" of the memories. Since no Corlan had ever committed this forbidden deed, he had no knowledge of what would happen. He hoped that at some point either his new surati would just give up and stop, or else he would be forced to leave whenever the boy was old enough to survive on his own. He pondered whether at some point the boy might become too old to even accept the surati. Even with his vague ideas and lack of knowledge, he was so delusional that his ridiculous plan made sense to him. He was sure it would work somehow.

Straf considered that mnet fruit was good for babies, and he planned on using that as a substitute for mother's milk. However, he did not realize that the raw fruit is unpalatable for babies and even dangerous unless its composition is altered by the surati.

He carefully harvested some mnet without directly touching it (for fear of spreading the surati to it), and he managed to grind some up. Finally, after much effort, he was able to get some into the baby's mouth without directly touching either the fruit or the baby. He was horrified to find that the baby was not willing to eat it. Whenever he forced it into the baby, it only caused choking, spitting, and ear-piercing screams.

The helpless baby could perhaps have physically survived without the memories, if only he had the care and milk of his mother, or at least some food he could digest and some kindness in the form of warm cuddling and the loving touch of a parent. Yet there in the mountains, he had no suitable food and no physical contact from his father, because of the wicked man's decision to not transmit the memories.

Since no Corlan had ever died, the deranged father never even considered that his baby might die. He spent hours, and then days, searching for something the baby would eat. The baby's perpetual screaming and crying drove him mad with rage. Nothing he tried was accepted. Because he thought that the baby would eventually get hungry enough to eat something, he tried over and over with several foods, always without directly touching the baby or the food. Out of weakness, eventually the baby's screams were reduced to only moans, yet Straf mistook this for progress.

Baby S'tael died after only about three days. It was the first Corlan death in all their long history. In a way, S'tael had, in fact, been murdered by his father through the neglect of necessary care that the kidnapping had forced upon the child.

At first Straf mistook death for sleep. Then he noticed that the baby was not breathing. This perplexed him for some time. For several hours he kept hoping the baby would stir. After almost a whole day, he was finally able to recall something from his degraded long-term memory. It was some detail about the eldest Corlan visiting another world, a place cursed by sin and plagued by death.

Finally Straf comprehended what had happened. He thought, *My son is dead. I am the cause. I am death.*

After Straf knew that the baby was dead, in heartbroken shock he finally decided to touch his son. He kissed the cold forehead. He kissed each quiet cheek. As he wept over the infant, his surati-filled tears dropped onto the baby's ashen face. Straf held the little body and stroked tiny lips that would never laugh or speak. He laid the child back down, and paced around for a while in dismay.

Then he slowly said out loud, "I am the Ettosedondi."

In sullen self-contempt he decided that if his son could die, he could die as well. In utter despair he took his son's dead body, and carried it to the top of a high, steep cliff. There he leaped to his own death, holding the baby all the way to the rocks below. The second death in all the long history of the Corlan was the Ettosedondi himself, yet the destruction he had caused was only beginning.

Just because a Corlan sins and dies does not mean the surati microbes die. Quite the contrary. God's design for the surati was for them to accommodate their sinless Corlan host in endless service. The very concept of death was incompatible with their divinely given charge and purpose. Straf's own surati were confused, but they were not the real problem. The global threat would come from the new surati that were intended for baby S'tael, whose tiny body lay crushed in the arms of his father.

Straf's corpse, broken upon the rocks at the base of the cliff, became a bitter fountain of new, unfulfilled surati that multiplied at an alarming rate, spreading in all directions and eating every substance they could to gain the needed elements for more replication of themselves.

Unable to find a *living* child who could serve as their host, they consumed the dead bodies of both Straf and S'tael, and then they began to spread out across the mountainside. They would not stop spreading and eating because they could not find their home. Sset was now firmly under the curse of Straf's sin.

The Ettosedondi was not the only source of unfulfilled surati. Everywhere his wife searched, she spread unfulfilled surati. *Straf* suspected that her husband had gone into the mountains, and so she searched there until she eventually collapsed from exhaustion and dehydration. Her body was smeared with the pink surati membrane, and her clothing was eaten by it. There on the mountainside, she died in the night. Her valiant effort to find her son and her sincere desire to transfer the memories were honored by God. The unfulfilled surati consumed her dead body and then continued to spread.

The microbes from both husband and wife had combined by the time the plague was discovered. A family that had gone into the mountains for a camping trip saw a massive swath of blighted terrain covered with a visible, pink gel of surati. Nothing was left uneaten anywhere it had spread. Every bit of vegetation was consumed, along with some inanimate matter. The peninsula where the Corlan reside was already cut off by the surati.

The family literally ran until they reached the outskirts

of the Corlan dwelling places. In fear and panic they reported what they had found.

In the Corlan language (which we will translate), the gasping family told everyone in the area, "The Ettose-dondi has come! Everywhere the surati spreads, there is no plant life remaining! We saw a large area where everything was consumed. Even portions of the soil were eaten away! It is coming!"

When word of this reached the Elders, they convened to pray and discuss the matter.

The eldest, Shao, told the others, "The trying time of judgment has finally come upon our world. Our people have never known lack of food or fear of death. Now that these terrible things have been unleashed among us, the courage and faith of every Corlan will be tested. Our true hearts will be revealed. If we must die, then let us die as godly Corlan, trusting in God for resurrection and not giving in to fear and doubt. Be strong. Be courageous. Now is the time to make known your love of God and your trust in Him."

The Corlan scientists were assembled to try to devise plans to slow down the onslaught of the unfulfilled surati. A few hoped to stop it entirely. Some came up with plans for firewalls (attempts to insulate the population from the plague with ditches filled with flammable fuels, which were then lit on fire). These plans were implemented, and they slowed its approach somewhat, but in each attempt eventually the surati would get through. Other scientists sought to devise acids that could destroy the surati, which could be poured from above by aerial vehicles. However, the acids were simply another way of slowing the surati, as they could not destroy enough of the substance, and the chemicals were eventually consumed by the surati as fuel for replication. Some scientists suggested contriving some type of biological weapon that could stop the unfulfilled surati, even though all efforts to devise such a weapon would likely have destroyed the normal surati living in all of them. However, none of those plans were viable, and their efforts were eventually abandoned.

The Corlan kind found itself trapped between the vast Ssettian ocean and a sea of aggressive surati. There were not enough aerial vehicles for an evacuation, and, worse, the flight range of their vehicles was not far enough to get past either the water or the surati.

As terror took hold in the Corlan population, the healthy surati within some began to malfunction, and their memories stopped being recorded by the microbes. In some of the younger Corlan that were still maturing, their ancestral memories stopped being retranslated for them. All of this added to the overwhelming sense of panic and confusion. A selfish mindset of "each must fend for himself" began to develop. It was intensely tragic.

The Ssettian animals began to die of starvation. The desperate Corlan, who had never before eaten animal meat, began to slaughter the remaining Ssettian creatures to eat them for food. This sustained them for a while, but many Corlan died in this effort because they tried to eat Ssettian creatures whose bodies contained toxic elements of which none was aware prior to the crisis.

Within a few days the populations of various Ssettian animals were reduced to almost nothing. Then the Corlan people began to starve to death. One by one they fell. As food supplies grew more and more scarce, the first instances of Corlan violence were witnessed.

As the unfulfilled surati spread across their world, the hearts of all the Corlan were revealed. Thousands abandoned all faith in God and became savages. Even some of the Elders gave way to panic, fear, and doubt. The Corlan were not only stealing food from one another, but some were actually killing one another for purposes of self preservation. Cannibalism became a reality. Their long-standing, peaceful paradise had been undone in only a short time.

CHAPTER XI

Ark of Safety

afety was not something that the Corlan had
ever needed to seek out, but the chaos caused by
the surati of the Ettosedondi changed everything. Most of the Corlan lost all faith in God. In sheer
panic they became very sinful. Only a handful of the
Corlan continued to trust in God. These were the few
that refused to give in. Over the course of the trial, God
took note of each and every Corlan that died without sin.

In the final days of the microbiotic siege, only 37 of
the remaining Corlan were willing to die honorably
without resorting to violence or surrendering to doubt
against God. Of them, 24 were murdered by demented
Corlan savages who literally ate them as food. The
remaining few were quietly gathered by Shao and hidden

away as part of a clandestine operation upon which the survival of their kind depended. Counting Shao, the eldest couple, a total of 13 Corlan were hidden away in an underground cavern that had been set aside as a kind of top-secret ark of safety.

We must now reveal to our reader that which had been kept concealed from all the Corlan. Shortly before the crisis, Shao had been commanded by God to secretly use a certain place to hold Ssettian plants, animals, and food. This secluded, unknown cavern was accessible only from a waterway. Our readers that are Christian will surely find undertones of our Lord's burial in the fact that the place was underground, and perhaps even more undertones of water baptism in the fact that the cavern could be entered only by walking through a waterfall.

Shao (the husband) was a leader who had never faced a real crisis until this time. Yet our reader must remember that no leader of our world ever had such a long time to prepare for his moment to lead through crisis. Shao had lived for well over a million days knowing all the while that one day he would witness the demise of his people. Over that time, as his kind slowly grew from two to many thousands, he lovingly adored and guided all the offspring, while always knowing that an atrocious trial would eventually reveal which of them truly loved God and which did not. He was an immensely kind soul, yet he had been shaped for this moment by both his position and the knowledge he carried. At the core, his kindness was undergirded by a strength that was not to be underestimated.

In the months leading up to the end, God had spoken to this eldest couple, revealing the location of the cavern. Shao had then worked by night to carry food and plants into the cavern. A phosphorescent Ssettian lichen covered the cavern's interior, which provided light by which to see (and to sustain the plants temporarily). In the final days, God aided Shao in collecting young animals with their potential mates, which he secretly smuggled into the cavern. Finally, a tiny handful of honorable Corlan (and their newest offspring) were the last creatures to be taken to the cavern under the cover of darkness. Shao first hid his own wife and their most recent offspring (from the most recent C'alimnet), a baby girl named *C'lou*.

As the Corlan dwelling places became a place of terror both by day and by night, the Lord guided Shao to certain of his offspring that were loyal to God and determined to die honorably. Shao smuggled these precious few families to the cavern. They had to be careful to avoid being found by cannibals. The rescues happened over the course of two nights.

The first family that was located and saved was Tap, in which the husband was a first-generation descendent of Shao, and the wife was of the second generation.

The Corlan dwelling places were structures of great beauty. Their lines were highly refined, and the details were very delicate. They were the natural result of an ancient art of architecture that had not ever been forced to account for decay, war, destruction, or abandonment. Even simple elements like crown molding were hand carved with intricate beauty. Ethereal, fragile lattices and gossamer arches that had taken hundreds of days to carve, and which were intended for enjoyment across hundreds or thousands more cam, were now abandoned, or smashed, or burned with fire.

As Shao moved furtively through the silent, empty Corlan homes, the Lord nudged him toward Tap's home, which seemed abandoned. There Shao found signs that intruders had previously been there and evidence of a struggle. As he walked across the stone floor of the dwelling, he called out his son's name. Finally he heard a sound like stone scraping against stone, and he turned to see a portion of the floor being moved out of its place. Up from beneath came Tap and his wife, along with their most recent offspring, *B'rei* (a baby girl). They were already somewhat emaciated, and they were very relieved to see Shao.

"You have found grace in the Lord's sight," Shao told them (in the Corlan language, of course). "Come with me to a place of safety prepared by the Lord through me."

While they were on their way, the Lord spoke to Shao

again, leading them to the home of Karq, a couple in which the wife was a first-generation descendent of Shao, and the husband was of the second generation. Their dwelling also appeared to be abandoned. They searched the rooms inside while Tap stood watch outside. After finding nothing in the main building, they began to search the other structures of the estate.

In the distance, they heard yelling and sounds of violence, so they ceased from calling Karq's name aloud. When Shao opened the door of a storage building, suddenly Karq (the husband) called out from within.

"If you intend us harm, then you will face the judgment of God for your actions," he said in despair. He was hiding inside with his wife and their new baby boy, whose name was T'anah.

"We bring good news," Shao replied, "You have found grace in the Lord's sight—"

At that moment, the angry voices they had detected in the distance were heard again, but this time they were very close, perhaps even in front of the main dwelling.

Tap came into the moons' light near them and whispered, "We are about to be discovered."

Shao quickly urged everyone to enter into the storage building, and they closed the door from within. They huddled quietly and prayed without speaking.

A number of deranged Corlan began to search the house and the area around it. They were among those who had already become cannibals. They were fighting among themselves while they looked through every building in the complex.

Suddenly the door to the storage building was opened, and a single light shined in. In what could only be described as a miracle, somehow the male Corlan staring straight at them did not even see them. He simply turned and went away. His body and clothing were stained with blood.

As he left, he murmured (apparently to himself), "There is no God. The memories are a lie."

They remained still, not even shutting the door, until the sounds of the intruders faded into the night.

Shao then led the little band into the wood, and finally they reached the waterfall that was the entrance to the cavern. He stayed there with everyone until the next night.

Karq's baby boy, T'anah, was a little more gaunt than *B'rei* (Tap's daughter), but all three of the hidden babies were healthy enough to survive, now that their mothers had access to food. The famished families thankfully partook of the provisions that Shao had hidden away.

That same night, on the far side of the Corlan dwelling places, a terrible tragedy was unfolding for Tav, a couple in which the wife was a third-generation descendent of Shao. She was Tap's granddaughter, born to his son, Swov.

The Tav family had been hiding with their baby daughter, *Z'aey*, in the wood near the outskirts of the dwelling places. They had starved nearly to the point of death, when the husband (a fourth-generation descendent) finally snapped. He departed from his starving wife and dying child for a long time, and then he returned with something.

"I found us something to eat," he said.

His wife looked and saw a Corlan body part, putrid and bloody. It was barely recognizable as part of a leg.

"No," she said, "I will not eat that. I would rather die."

Enraged, he shouted, "You *will* eat it, or you are killing our daughter!" Then he added (as though he had realized a terrible, potential double meaning for his words), "You cannot nourish her if you are dead!"

He began to devour the raw flesh. His wife pondered the possible outcomes, and in desperation she chose the only one that she could consider as acceptable to God. She was resolute that her daughter must not ever be nourished by the flesh of another Corlan. At best it would only delay death for a little while, but at what cost? It would poison her relationship with God for eternity. Besides, consuming the putrid flesh could sicken them and hasten death. It simply was not worth it to give in.

Tav arose and acted as though she had succumbed to his wishes. She stepped away for a moment as if to fetch something, and she then struck him on the back of the head with the largest rock she could lift. He collapsed and lost consciousness. Then she took up her baby girl, and with all the strength she could muster, she made her way to her parents' home. Their estate was far off the beaten path, away from most of the Corlan dwellings and nearer to the ocean.

As she approached, they were caught in a trap that her father had set to catch cannibals. Both *Tav* and her daughter were scooped up in a very large net, which suspended them above the ground. By the time her father found them the next morning, *Tav* had died of starvation and dehydration. Her baby daughter was still alive, but just barely. Swov carefully cut the net down and took his granddaughter into their home. While his wife cared for both their baby and *Tav's* baby, Swov spent that day working to cover his daughter's dead body with rocks. As darkness fell, he was too weak and tired to reset the trap. Back inside, they prayed that no wickedness would find them that night. Far away, at that same moment, Shao and Tap were setting out on another rescue mission.

Shao told Tap, "The Lord has shown me that this is the last night of rescue. Almost all the faithful Corlan are already dead. We are to rescue the last ones. It is your son, Swov, and his family."

They left the cavern and made their way through the wood, finally reaching the dwelling places. An eerie silence greeted them. It was both a relief and an alarming reminder of the swift downfall of their people. Some of the area was overrun with surati, and they had to be very careful in their going, lest they accidentally carry some of the surati back to the cavern. They made it safely though the concentration of homes. Soon they could smell the ocean, and they heard distant waves pounding out a rhythmic psalm that was somehow above and utterly unaware of the tragedy that had befallen the Corlan.

When they finally reached the Swov residence, they were spared from the net because *Tav* had sprung the trap, and Swov had not yet reset it. They stood at the base of the rather tall building that Swov had built for his home, and they called out to them.

Tap shouted, "Swov! This is your father and your father's father. We have come to rescue you!"

On a balcony above them, a voice in the darkness shouted back, "Praise be to God! We will come down!"

As Swov and his family joined them, Shao said, "Come with us to a place of safety prepared by the Lord through your eldest."

Shao and Tap were glad to see Swov's most recent off-spring, R'ei, a baby boy who was conceived at the most recent C'alimnet. However, they were pleasantly surprised to see an additional baby, wrapped up in blankets.

"Who is this?" Shao inquired.

"Sire, this is your great-granddaughter, *Z'aey*. Her

mother, *Tav*, perished while trying to get her to us. We don't know what might have happened to the father."

Shao prayed for a moment, and then said, "We are not to seek him out. We must get back to the cavern."

Their meager existence inside the cavern was cramped, damp, chilly, and uncomfortable, but at least they were alive. Outside the cavern, the last remaining Corlan were either killing each other or dying of starvation while cursing God.

The little remnant knew their only hope was God. Unless the Lord somehow brought salvation, eventually either they would run out of food or the plague of unfulfilled surati would somehow find them and wipe out their remaining food. They needed a miracle to avoid death by starvation.

As they sat and talked, Shao said, "God would not have provided this place of safety for us if He did not intend to preserve our kind and our memories. We must trust in Him. I believe that somehow He will come and help us."

They all made a pact with each other, and with God, to remain honorable until the end. If they died before seeing God's salvation, so be it. They vowed to each other that regardless of whatever might happen, they would not give way to doubt, fear, or panic, nor turn on each other. They swore to protect one another's young children as if they were their own. Even though the orphaned baby girl, *Z'aey*, was too young to understand, they pledged to her that they would care for her as if she were their own.

"How do you think the Lord might help us?" asked *Karq* (the wife).

Her husband said, "I don't know. I cannot imagine how."

Tap said, "The Lord has the power to stop the surati. If He had intended to, surely He could already have done so. He is allowing the surati to judge the Corlan. Only when the judgment is complete will He reveal the solution. We simply need to wait, trust, and hope."

Swov (the wife) was sensitive to the Lord, and gifted with dreams. She spoke up.

"I have been having the same dream each night. At first I thought it was simply because my surati are confused. In the dream, I see a baby. He is a son not born of Corlan descent. He is a child not born of our world," she said.

Shao smiled and said, "A child not born of this world. This is a marvelous thing. Our hope is renewed."

So little light from the outside penetrated through the waterfall that they had trouble discerning day from night. Much time passed, and yet nothing happened to save them. Their hope flickered like a candle about to burn out. They spent their days caring for their young and laboring to feed the animals. They spent their evenings in prayer. Karq (the husband) was having a tough time with fear. His surati stopped recording his memories, and he began to suffer erratic outbursts. Afterward, he would always calm himself and pledge to do better. Regardless, the level of concern within the cramped cavern was slowly rising toward a boiling point.

After many days and nights, one evening Tap noticed that the glowing lichen around the cavern's entrance was being eaten by the surati. He came running to tell the others.

"The surati of the Ettosedondi have found the cavern."

They looked at each other somberly. They were desperate to hold onto hope that somehow God's salvation was at hand. From their natural point of view, it seemed the end was near. It would require only a short time for the surati to take over the cavern.

CHAPTER XII

A Son Given

For some portions of the Millennial Kingdom age, Daniel and Tess weren't able to spend as much time together as usual, but there was so much to do, and their areas of specialty did not always overlap. They were both involved in so many different tasks, and they were helping so many people. Regardless, they had all of eternity ahead of them to catch up with one another, so there was no sense of regret or any reason to be concerned about their relationship.

The day that Daniel was shot by James Therrill, a mortal, Tess dropped everything and instantly reverted back into her prior role of wife as she checked him over. She also helped with the care of Sensba, the young man who was grazed by the bullet that had passed through Daniel.

Sensba was one of many mortal men (both young and old) that Daniel and other immortal men were helping and mentoring. Likewise, Tess and other immortal women were involved in helping and mentoring many mortal women. The immortals themselves no longer cared about gender or related issues, but because their mortal charges cared about such things, they took this into account. Many mortal men would happily allow themselves to be mentored by an immortal that they perceived as a man, yet would never allow it by someone they perceived as a woman. The same was true going the other way also. (If the reader was not aware of this fact while previously reading Daniel's journal, then the reader may have wondered why the group that Daniel and Steed mentored seemed like a "guys only" club. It was indeed a group of only men, and that was a deliberate choice.)

Suffice it to say that the would-be assassin was not able to kill an immortal with his bullet, and he was later won over to God by Daniel and Steed.

We won't take time here to retell the whole story. Our fond reader is encouraged to read the account in Daniel's own journal, published previously under the title *New Immortal*.

As the end of the Millennial Kingdom age drew near, the Lord called for Tess.

When she came into His presence, He said, "Tess,

there is a crisis about to occur on a world in another universe—another space-time. What is happening there requires your help, and Daniel's help as well.

"In the meantime, a crisis is coming on the Earth that also requires Daniel's involvement. Once I tell you what is happening on the other world, called Sset, and once you know the details of my plan to help them, you will find it difficult to remain focused here. You will scarcely be able to pay attention to what is happening now. The same would be true of Daniel. For that reason, he must not be told yet, or else he would not be able to concentrate and fulfill his role in the coming crisis on the Earth."

"Yes, Lord. I understand," Tess answered.

"Tess, you are to become a mother."

Tess struggled to comprehend the Lord's words.

"But how—?" she murmured.

"This is an easy thing, is it not?" He said, smiling. Then He added, "This offspring will be yours and Daniel's. This will be a child born out of due season. He will be a son given to preserve alive a tiny remnant of a once-noble people on the world of Sset. They are called the Corlan.

"Unlike Adam, the first couple here on the Earth, which sinned and brought a curse of death upon this world, the first couple on Sset, whose name is Shao, did not ever sin. Over a long, regal history, they and their many children have lived in sinless innocence, enjoying the paradise that I created for them.

"However, soon the wicked one that I foretold will come upon them. He will sin against Me and against his own people, and he will bring a curse of sin and death upon his world. Out of many thousands, only a handful will remain. I am going to spare them alive. I will do this with your help."

Over the hours that followed, the Lord explained much of the history, culture, and biological details of the Corlan. Once Tess finally understood why they were going to need a child who could accept the rampant microbes and who would, therefore, become Corlan by virtue of receiving the memories, the Lord finally began to speak to Tess about motherhood.

"This is related to your visit to the past long ago," He said. "You remember the trip."

"Yes, Lord," she said. "I visited the past and saw myself as a child."

"That is how you will become a mother—by visiting the past," the Lord told her. "You must journey to your prior self and retrieve what is required."

The Lord explained the plan to her in detail. He again emphasized that she must not tell Daniel yet.

"Is there anyone in whom I can confide?" she pleaded.

The Lord smiled and said, "You may confide in Anna. She must not tell her son. He cannot know of this until the crisis on the Earth is past. Even though she is Daniel's mother and this will be her own grandchild, she must keep the matter secret until after the judgment."

Tess translated herself to the mansion of Anna Talbot. After a long talk with her, Anna was brought in on the secret.

Tess told her, "You see now why I begged to be able to confide in someone. Keeping something like this a complete secret was too much for me."

"I am awed by God's majestic plan and His wisdom," Anna said. "I will keep the secret, but it seems like too much for both of us. I never imagined such a thing in my fondest dreams."

Tess and Anna had always been so close that they thought they could never be any closer. Yet this shared secret drew them nearer still. Tess began spending all of her spare time with Anna at her mansion. Together they studied the Corlan language. Tess mastered the basics of it. Sometimes they daydreamed about the baby boy that was to come.

One day while they were together, they were surprised by the sudden appearance of Daniel. As he came in, so focused upon the growing crisis related to their world, these two of his dearest friends looked upon him with love, struggling to keep a secret that burned within them.

He told them about some anti-immortal rhetoric that had just been broadcasted on a show hosted by someone named Mary Heger. They talked for a while.

Finally Anna told him, "Son, just have faith because God's going to work it all out."

In her mind she had an entirely different set of circumstances in view, going all the way back to the young couple's earliest days of being childless and trying to hold onto hope because of a mysterious promise from an enigmatic lady that no one seemed to know. Daniel had no way to know the broader context of her words, so, to him, the advice sounded humorous. He began to smile. For a moment Anna and Tess wondered if they had somehow given away something of their secret.

"What are you smiling about?" Anna asked him.

Daniel said, "Only a mother would tell her immortal, glorified son—who serves the Lord continually—that he needs to 'have faith because God's going to work it all out.' Mama, you know I have no doubts regarding whatever God has planned. It just gives me pause to think when I see a man who actually used a gun to attempt murder walking around free and testifying on a public broadcast. I know God is up to something. I'm just wondering what it is."

With a sigh of relief that their secret was still safe, Tess resisted the urge to say what she was thinking, which was, *Oh, Danny boy! He's up to something indeed, and you can't even begin to imagine what it is.*

Instead all she said was, "I can see why you wanted to talk. Likewise, let's consider Sensba's feelings. He's not only young in the Lord, he's just young, period. Has anyone gotten with him about this yet?"

"Yes," Daniel said. "Steed was with Sensba when the announcement of Therrill's release was made public and also when the show was broadcasted."

Tess said, "Good. Sensba really looks up to you two. Nevertheless, I think I will go look in on him, too."

With that she kissed both Daniel and Anna goodbye, and she teleported out.

Daniel hugged his mother and said, "Mama, I love you forever. I need some time alone to think. I'll see you soon."

Then he translated himself back to the Earth, to his favorite remote mountain top, and sat in silence.

The two immortals that loved him the most had a secret larger than any secret in the history of secrets, and they had to keep it in. He was oblivious to it, as he focused on the issues at hand.

One day, as Tess was working on the plan, remembering specific dates and pondering when and where to go, the room suddenly brightened as the Lord appeared.

"Lord," she said, "I think I have both dates plotted: the first date is when I had my emergency surgery after the accident. That is when to retrieve my ova. The second date is when Daniel and I were married. I can retrieve his seed from one of the nights of our honeymoon."

"You have questions though," the Lord said.

"Yes, Lord," Tess responded. "I need some detail help. What actually happened to my organs that were removed that day? Where in the hospital should I retrieve them?"

"The organs taken from you remained in the operating room for a short time, and they were later carried to Pathology, which was a laboratory area in the basement of the hospital," the Lord said. "After they were examined there, they were eventually thrown in with everything else that was classified as 'infectious waste.' Finally they were destroyed by incineration. How symbolic that the culture of that day would call precious seed 'waste,' and how appropriate that we shall be saving it from that fate.

"Tess, you will need to do more than plan the dates. You will need to plan the time. There was a period after your surgery when your organs were left unattended in the operating room. You should be there between 8:47 and 8:48 PM."

"Yes, Lord," Tess replied.

"Tess, there is one other reason I came," the Lord said. "This is the time for you to tell Daniel."

"But, Lord," Tess stuttered, "I thought you said—?"

"It is not time for you to tell him here and now. This," the Lord answered, while pointing to her date notations, "is the time for you to tell the Daniel of that day. It is time to give him the promise that you will be a mother someday."

Slowly the truth settled in.

"I was the lady dressed in white!" Tess exclaimed.

"Yes," the Lord confirmed, "Wait until the news of your childlessness has been delivered to you and to Daniel. Then you may tell him that you are going to recover, and that you are going to be a mother. In the days ahead, as you struggle to keep this secret from our Daniel now, you can at least take comfort in knowing that you have told Daniel then!"

Tess thanked the Lord profusely.

Tess carefully calculated the first jump. It was not yet time to retrieve the ovum or sperm, but she was glad for this jump to visit Daniel of the past—both for the chance to practice time-jumping and for the chance to see Daniel and tell him the promise.

Tess arrived a week early. The realization that she could actually see her parents alive was overwhelming. It occurred to her she may have subconsciously skewed the trip just to make that happen. She teleported into the old house, but remained out of phase so she would be invisible.

Her mother, May, was in the kitchen. Her father, Perry, was in the family room. The Tess of that day was upstairs at the time, trying on the cap and gown. The household was focused in a major way on details pertaining to her commencement. They had ordered too many invitations. A stack of unused ones, along with their envelopes, were still sitting on the coffee table. Tess's mother was on the phone with a caterer. Her father was looking at yearbooks and reminiscing.

The urge to materialize—to hug them, kiss them, warn them, preach to them, and help them somehow—became more than she could bear. She realized anew why such trips were dangerous, as she reminded herself of the risks of corrupting the timeline.

At that moment her dad suddenly stopped and looked up, as though he could see her. Tess double-checked to be sure she was out of phase. He was up and moving toward her. He passed through where she was, and then pulled a box out of the closet behind her.

Tess knew that even if she came into normal phase and materialized, still it would not achieve any good goal. Only harm and damage would come from trying to change the past. She tore herself away emotionally and finally withdrew from the house.

When she arrived back in her own time again, she sensed that she had passed a major test. Tess decided to wait a few days before trying again.

Tess again carefully calculated the jump. This time she got it right. She arrived on the sixth day after the accident. It was only the second day after she had regained consciousness. Daniel was outside of the intensive care unit, waiting to be allowed in to visit her. Tess stood across from Daniel, out of phase, of course. As she waited for the right time, she looked upon her beloved. He was a skinny teenage boy; just a kid really. She looked at him and thought, *He's such a good kid, Tess. You should have gone easier on him.*

At that moment a doctor passed by. He had just left her room in the intensive care unit. He was the one who had drawn the short straw. He was the one who had to inform her of the bad news of her childlessness.

She waited for Daniel to go in and see the young Tess.

This won't take long, she thought, *I'm probably telling him to leave right about now.*

Tess looked up and down the hall. There was no one in sight, so she came into normal phase, which made her visible. Right on time, Daniel came through the ICU doors again. He was praying under his breath. As Tess looked into the face of this teenage boy who was so concerned, she could not help but be concerned as well.

"Daniel, everything is going to be fine," she said, "Tess is going to be OK, and *one day she will be a mother.* Just trust God about everything."

Daniel nodded his head and asked, "Do I know you?"

"Yes!" she said, laughing, "Eventually you'll figure out how you know me."

As Daniel looked toward the doors of the intensive care unit for a moment, Tess glanced down the hall. No one was in sight. She took advantage of the moment and teleported out.

As Daniel turned back to where she had been standing, he said, "I know God can do miracles—"

Tess was already gone. The nurse that approached Daniel after that, to ask about the woman in white, had actually seen Tess from another time-jump, which had yet to occur. It was to be a time-jump to an earlier moment.

The crisis on Sset and the crisis on Earth were coming to a head at almost the same time. Because Tess had no frame of reference for making the jump to that realm, she had to simply trust in God for how it would happen, and there was to be no effort at all to adjust the exit on that end of the portal to any time other than their present.

As the Millennial Kingdom age was drawing to a close, Tess tried to make herself forget about Sset and Corlans and even about her baby to come so she could try to focus on helping with the rescue effort that was to happen on the Earth. She found it so difficult to concentrate on anything that she completely understood why the Lord had prevented them from telling Daniel. She attended the big debate and supported Daniel, but her mind was really elsewhere.

That was certainly a day of mixed feelings. Following the debate, she watched with joy as Dr. Jumoke Kasiya and Mary Heger were converted and filled by God's Spirit and baptized. Then she and Daniel and all the other immortals groaned as they sensed the release of demonic spirits that resulted from the wickedness of mortal men who had rejected the Lord's rule over them.

The time had come for Tess to make the two very important time-jumps. She arrived on time for the first one, and watched as her Aunt Mildred and Uncle Percy waited with Daniel and Anna Talbot. The Tess of that day was in emergency surgery. It was fascinating to real-ize that while they sat in their present, without any sig-nificant sense of perspective, she was watching them from her present, with over a thousand years of perspec-tive. Just down the hall, a group of dedicated medical professionals fought to save the life of a young girl. While she was out of phase, Tess slipped into the operat-ing room, to wait for the right moment.

The swollen, traumatized Tess of that day was sewn up and wheeled out into the recovery area. Exhausted doc-tors and nurses congratulated one another. They were somewhat more confident that she would survive than they dared let on when talking later with the family. It was 8:47 PM. As the last nurse left the room, Tess came into normal phase, and collected some of "herself" from the pan where they had placed her internal organs.

She placed the organ tissue that contained her ova

into a container that she had brought with her. She slipped out of the operating room, and then went down the hall toward the waiting area, thinking she might catch one more glimpse of her family and friends.

She was passed in the hall by a nurse who was just coming on duty. The nurse was perplexed to see someone other than hospital staff coming out of the area of the operating rooms. As soon as the lady passed her, Tess realized that she had forgotten to go back out of phase. Just before the lady turned around to ask her if she could help her find where she should be, Tess teleported out.

In the second time-jump, Tess teleported back to the second night of her honeymoon with Daniel. After both Daniel and Tess from that time were asleep, she obtained what she needed, which had resulted from marriage bed activities.

The great Day of Judgment for humanity was finally past, and a new group of redeemed humans had just become immortal, while many people had been judged without ever accepting the Lord's offer of salvation.

Tess found Daniel. He and Steed were busy talking to Sensba, James, and several other new immortals.

She told him, "Daniel, time is rather tight, and so I cannot explain it all right now, but I have unbelievably good news. As you know, I've been working on a secret project for the Lord. There is a world, called Sset, where a plague is wiping out everything, and they need a child—a human child—in order to save their world. The Lord has decided that the human child is to come from you and I. I am to be a mother. You are to be a father. I have already journeyed to the past and retrieved my ova and your seed."

It took several full seconds for her words to register. Then came complete surprise. Daniel's mouth fell open. He drew in a breath as though he would speak.

Tess said, "Don't ask. I will explain it all later. Right now, it's time for you to come with me to see the Lord."

Then, to all the friends nearby, she said, "All are welcome to come along! Congratulations are in order! *It's a boy!*"

Tess made a motion with her hands, and everyone gathered close. She opened up a portal and teleported them to where the Lord had their new baby. The Blaylocks and many others were already there waiting. There was a ball of light hanging on nothing in the middle of a room that had no doors or windows. The Lord reached into that ball of light, and pulled out a perfect baby boy. The child had neither umbilical cord nor navel. He was completely content, and beautiful beyond words. His eyelids were half closed, and he yawned.

Daniel put his head into his hands as he tried to understand. Tess wept for joy while reaching for the baby. If our fond reader has ever witnessed any brand new mother cradle her baby for the first time, then there is no need for the author to expend pages trying to explain a moment that cannot be described with words. Daniel looked on with sheer awe.

After holding the baby for a few minutes, she turned to Daniel and said, "Please allow me to give you what was already yours."

As Daniel held the tiny life, he gave up trying to understand how or why. Then he, too, wept for joy. Never was a new father so happy. In those intensely joyous moments, their baby's heartbeat became the official measurement of time.

Suddenly the Lord said, "Tess, it is time to go. *Now.*"

Tess retrieved the baby from Daniel and told him, "You're to go, too. It's just you, me, and the baby. I'll explain as much as I can as soon as we can get a minute."

She held their new baby in both arms while holding onto Daniel with her finger tips. With the Lord's help, she formed a special portal that first took them out of space-time entirely, and then they looked on as two distinct pockets of space-time were laid side by side ahead of them. One was where they had come from, the other was where they were going. As Daniel and Tess looked around, they saw other universes as well. They were seeing things that even their fellow immortals had not ever seen. It was clear there were more available directions than any three-dimensional realm could afford. Tess then understood: It was as though they were within one cube of a tesseract in a four-dimensional place, and the other cubes all around them were paths to separate universes. It was a hypercube.

A tesseract, she thought. *You gotta be kidding me.*

Tap (the husband) had just run in to announce that the unfulfilled surati had discovered their ark of safety. The luminous lichen around the cavern's entrance was being replaced by darkness as it was consumed by the surati.

"The surati of the Ettosedondi have found the cavern."

He tried to not let a hint of despair show in his voice.

As they looked at each another, *Swov* (the wife) said, "Trust in the Lord. He will help us."

Karq (the husband) said, "The Lord promised us a resurrection. Perhaps that is how He will help us. We may die in the end."

Swov answered, "But what of my dream? Trust in the Lord. He will help us."

Karq picked up a sack of dried Trias fruit, and then suddenly tossed it away.

"What is it?" asked Shao.

Karq said, "It is covered with surati."

The seemingly long seconds that followed were the final moments of truth for the group. Long fingers of darkness were creeping toward them on all sides of the cavern. The only Corlan remaining on the moon world of Sset quietly wept, somberly worshipped God, and prayed for salvation, as the light in the cavern slowly faded. Some closed their eyes, as they could not bear to watch while death visibly approached.

Suddenly there was an odd sensation in the room. None of them had ever experienced anything like it. A palpable shockwave washed over them like an ocean wave made of air pressure and electricity. At the same moment, a new glow was added to the room. They looked up to see two people, a man and a woman, standing near them in the cavern. Both were dressed in white. The woman was holding something. The something was a newborn baby.

Then the woman spoke (in very good Corlan), "Tell us where the surati is."

Shao leaped to his feet. He picked up the sack of dried fruit and verified that it had surati on its surface.

"Here is some of the unfulfilled surati," he said.

"Show us how to administer it to our baby," she said.

"You are not Corlan?" he asked. "This baby is not born of our world?"

"That is true. We are not Corlan. Our baby is not born of this world. He has no surati within," she answered.

He suddenly took her hand, and rubbed the fruit sack against it. Then he did the same for the man.

"If you would give your baby to become Corlan and to receive the sacred memories, then you will save us and preserve our people," he said, "Rub your hands upon your baby. Give him the memories."

On their palms, Daniel and Tess had a strange substance that had come from the sack. They rubbed it onto their new baby son. As the surati sensed the living child it had found, a baby without any surati inside, an invisible signal was communicated to the entire colony of microbes across their world. Within seconds, the plague was stayed. All of the new surati not in contact with the baby quickly changed color and then dried up as it became inert. Finally all that was left of it was a flaky powder, lightly purple in color. The surati that were in contact with the baby soaked into his skin, and then they began to take up residence in their new home.

Their arrival was so gentle that it did not even wake the baby from his slumber. The addition of the surati apparently caused him no discomfort at all. A few minutes later, he gently stirred and became very hungry for mother's milk. Tess had to raise her voice to be heard over his strong cries.

"We have a little problem," Tess said in her excellent Corlan, "Although we were married long ago, we are both now—different. We are this baby's parents, yet I am not as I once was. I am not equipped to nurse my son."

"Do not worry," said *Shao* (the wife). "There are four mothers with newborns here. We can nurse your child, if that is acceptable."

As Tess handed the baby over to *"Aunt Shao"* (as she later came to be called), she turned to Daniel and said, "I know you don't speak Corlan, so I will explain all this later."

In *perfect* Corlan, Daniel answered, "What do you mean? I understood everything—"

"What?" she asked, "When— How do you know the Corlan language?"

Still speaking in perfect Corlan, Daniel said, "What language? I don't know any— Who was speaking in a Corlan language? I understood *everything*."

Tess shook her head and said, "These are the Corlan. I learned some of their language. We've been speaking in their language!"

"Well, it all made perfect sense to me," Daniel said, "The Lord must have blessed me with their language as a gift!"

Perfect Corlan, Tess thought. *You gotta be kidding me.*

Daniel, who was desperate to understand all that had happened, finally said his first words that were not in Corlan, "What on Earth just happened? Umm, wait. Scratch that. We're not on the *Earth* at all, are we? Where are we? What just happened?"

Tess smiled and said, "Not on Earth is right. Congratulations, new Daddy. I'll explain everything later. Right now, however, has it occurred to you that we have carried our new baby to an alien world and handed him over to an alien nanny, all before we even named him?"

Daniel stuttered and stammered, "Whoa. I'm— OK, this is—"

"Is it OK if we name him after my Daddy?" Tess asked.

"You don't want to name him after me?" Daniel replied.

"You'll always be around," Tess explained, "We don't need to name our baby after you in order to remember you. My Daddy is not with us. Is it OK?"

"Sure," Daniel said, "Perry Talbot it is."

"Perry *Daniel* Talbot," she corrected.

"I stand corrected," he replied. "Perry *Daniel* Talbot."

"But on Sset, they name a baby with a *dri* until he or she gets married, so his name would be—"

"P'erry! Remember? I know Corlan!"

"You sicken me."

"You're immortal. You cannot be sickened."

"Still."

"OK," Daniel said, "I want details! What on— Where are we again? What on *Sset* just happened!?"

The Corlan survivors started sorting through their supplies to see how much remained and how much had been eaten by the surati. They would later discover that the powdery, inert surati that covered all the landscape was to seeds and roots what kindling was to fire. It was better than any fertilizer Tess and Daniel had ever seen.

Shao gave waterproof garments to Daniel and Tess, and then he led them out through the waterfall to show them the Ssettian sky at night. No stars are visible from anywhere on Sset, because of the sedondi aspect of their universe. However, T'and dominates the night sky magnificently, and there are always a few of the 28 moons in sight, which makes for an impressive display, especially at night.

Daniel could not resist the urge to show off a little for Tess. He began pointing at things and giving their Corlan names. He named all of the moons that were in sight at the moment, and he was starting on other things when she interrupted him, good-naturedly.

"Hey! Enough, you big show-off!"

As the morning dawned, Daniel pointed to the glow strip.

"Trasedondi!" he said.

"You know," Tess said, "I think I have this figured out. The Lord knew that you would never be able to learn Corlan on your own, so He had mercy on you and gave it to you as a gift."

"Is that so? Is that *so?*" Daniel said. "No, I think you're just jealous over the fact that the Lord showed me a special kindness because of me being the last one to learn your big secret! Good job, by the way, on keeping the big secret. How long did you know?"

"Well, your Mom and I have known since—"

"What!? My Mama knew this and kept it from me! I can't believe it!"

"Oh, boy," Tess said. "Listen, technically, you were not the last to know. You were actually the first. I went back in time to tell you. Back in the hospital, that lady dressed in white was yours truly."

That little tidbit left Daniel with no comeback at all. As he stood there pondering the ramifications of her revelation to him, Tess opened the bag of dried fruit, pulled out a piece, and took a bite.

Daniel said, "So, what did you bring for lunch today?"

"Well, it tastes a little bit like grape jelly. Now if I could just find a loaf of bread and some peanut butter, we could have PB&J."

"Cool."

The End
Of Another Beginning

About the Chronicles:

Hi, I'm Doug Joseph, author of the Skyport Chronicles. I trust you enjoyed reading Book Two, and I encourage you to read all the books in the series, available (in both print and ebook editions) wherever books are sold. You can read free samples online at  SkyportChronicles.com. See the "Skyport Time Line" below to find where this book fits into the overall story arc. For the latest news on the series, see the publisher's website at WhiteStonePublishing.com, or to see what I'm up to, visit my blog at DougJoseph.net! By the way, as of the time of this publishing I am working on Book Four of the series! You're really going to love it!

Skyport Time Line:

New Immortal (Skyport Chronicles, Book One)

"Broadened my horizons...."
—**David S. Norris, Ph.D.**
*Best-selling Author, Professor of Bible &
Theology, Urshan Graduate School of
Theology, St. Louis, MO*

"Forget James Bond & Jason Bourne..."
—**Roy H. Williams**
*New York Times Bestselling Author,
"Wizard of Ads," Founder & President of
Wizard Academy, Austin, TX*

Daniel Talbot is a teleporting, spy-
chasing, miracle-working immortal
serving in the royal court of Jesus
during the Millennial Kingdom age.

YA Fiction | Christian | Futuristic | Sci-Fi | Prophecy

The Last Bye (Skyport Chronicles, Book Three)

"Just finished reading *The Last Bye*
to the children. It's even better than
[C.S. Lewis'] *A Horse and His Boy*!
The children are very upset that there
are no more in this series [yet].
These books are wonderful!"
—**Christina Li, BA, MA**
*Bestselling Author, Journalist, and
Inspirational Speaker*

While growing up on a distant world,
P'erry suffers heartache, makes friends,
discovers the Tirra (great flying
creatures), has breath-taking adventures,
and achieves crucial accomplishments
for the people of his world.

YA Fiction | Christian | Futuristic | Sci-Fi | Romance

Available wherever great books are sold.

www.ingramcontent.com/pod-product-compliance
Lightning Source LLC
Chambersburg PA
CBHW022114170626
46808CB00002B/723